CHEESE RUNNERS

CHEESE RUNNERS TRILOGY
BOOK ONE

BY
CHRIS A. JACKSON

ISBN 1-939837-12-X
ISBN-13 978-1-939837-12-7

Cover art by Brian King
© Jaxbooks Publishing

Acknowledgements

Thanks so much to Bryan King for the cover art and to Charles Crawford for the cover concept. Special thanks to Jeff Breslauer for the idea to produce the story as an audiobook, and for bringing my characters to life with his great voice work.

CHAPTER ONE

BUSTED

Record # KR29387/a. Transcript begins:

Music blared through the tiny, cluttered bridge of the *Limburger*. Old music. Roiling guitar riffs that rattled my eardrums and would have curled Mozart's curly hair climbed and fell with the barely intelligible lyrics.

Not my favorite, especially when I'm being shot at.

"Man, I hate it when she plays that stuff!"

I hated to agree with Turk on any subject involving taste, be it concerning food, drink, music, literature (like he *reads*), government, the opposite sex, or any combination thereof, but here and now I had to give his assessment the nod. I wasn't going to admit it, of course; I wasn't one to start dissing Kik's choice of music at a time like this. After all, she was trying to keep us alive.

A huge ball of white blossomed ahead of us and slightly to starboard—I often wonder about those ancient sailing terms that we still use in space vessels—and the shockwave expanded toward us. I estimated it at forty megatons or so, just a love tap, a wakeup call from our pursuers, something to let us know it could have been four hundred if they wanted it so, and right on our nose instead of a hundred klicks out. Well, at least that meant they wanted us alive; some consolation...

"Hope you've got your SPF one thousand on! That shockwave's gonna pack some rads!" That was Turk's idea of humor, about as good as it ever got.

"The shielding should soak up most of it." Probably not, but what's a little DNA damage between rival species. Oh, yeah, I forgot. We weren't *rivals* of the Farfnians, we were only peons, pests, flies in their ointment. I watched the fly-swatter approach in the form of a hyper-accelerated wave of radioactive dust. I thumbed the ship-wide intercom and said, "All hands, brace yourselves!"

I took my own advice and managed not to be tossed out of my seat.

Several ancient music disks, two coffee cups, and a foot massager fell to the deck from the pilot's console as the *Limburger* yawed with the shockwave. Turk let out a stream of profanity, but Kik was oblivious to the clatter. Of course, she couldn't have moved if she wanted to. It never ceases to amaze me how oblivious a pilot is with the sensor net on, but I guess that's why I'm captain and not pilot. The thought of that neuro-conducting membrane pressing against my flesh—*all* of my flesh, as in every square nanometer—gives me the creepy crawlies. Kik doesn't seem to mind it, though, and has often commented that an exhilarating flight was "better than sex." I'll have to take her word on that, too, since her idea of carnal relations is different than mine. Kik's a xenophile—poorly repressed shudder—and never misses an opportunity to…uh…go where no man, or woman, has gone before.

"I don't mind the music," I lied, cringing as another, more violent, shockwave sent a new cascade of paraphernalia clattering to the deck, "when we're not being shot at." That one had been behind and to port. They had us perfectly bracketed and could kill us at any time.

"Jeez, you gotta be kiddin' me, Harry!" Turk's voice was beginning to get on my nerves more than the ancient music. I thought about offering to let *him* pilot the *Limburger* the next time we got caught by a Farfnian patrol cruiser, but then reconsidered. He might take me up on the offer, and that would undoubtedly leave us cavorting around space in a ship so dented and dinged that no self-respecting planet would let us into a parking orbit. Or worse yet, he might take it personally and break my arm for me…again.

"TARGET CLOSING. DISTANCE ONE THOUSAND

KILOMETERS."

Okay, I hate computer voices. They bring back really bad memories for me that I don't care to relate at this particular time.

"Yeah, right! Like *they're* the freakin' target!"

"Cycle it, Turk!" Well, I guess the prospect of a broken arm was suddenly less daunting than listening to his complaints.

I really don't know why I put myself through situations like this. I mean, it wasn't like we had a Popsicle's™ chance in a supernova of outrunning the cruiser. The Farfnian ship was bigger, faster, better armed—We weren't armed at all. Well, not precisely *armed,* anyway—and more technologically advanced than our little courier-class freighter. That's the trouble with the Farfnians, they're *always* bigger, better, faster, and smarter than us. Us meaning the whole human race, not just myself and present company. Well, maybe *especially* not myself and present company.

Seventy-five years ago they had conquered Earth's combined military might in just two hours and sixteen minutes. Who knew they could just *turn off* every electrical thing on the planet? Then they had the gall to insist that we stop killing one another and form a single planetary government. I mean *really*! We told them that we were *quite* capable of handling our *own* disputes, thankyouverymuch!

The asteroid they dropped between the West Bank and Jerusalem was about twenty miles in diameter. The Dead Sea is now Mediterranean beachfront property.

Point taken.

The Unified Earth Government was then informed that all of our problems were hereby solved: no hunger, no pollution, no war, no crime, no addiction, no unemployment, no disease, no old age, and no money.

How *dare* they!

They pumped so much foreign aid into bringing our sniveling little backwater planet up to technological speed with the rest of the galaxy that every human on the planet was left with their mouth hanging open for the next ten years.

They have no idea how many humans they pissed off.

The rich were mad because their money was worth less than wallpaper, the poor were mad because they couldn't blame the rich for being poor, the workers were mad because they were out of work, the unemployed were mad because their benefits were cancelled, the disabled were mad because their disabilities were no longer disabling—Modern prosthetics are wonderful. I've got one myself—and the government was mad because it no longer wielded any real power to make everyone miserable. The entire world economy was worth about as much as a 1972 Dodge Dart with no hubcaps, simply because nothing that Earth could produce was worth anything on the Galactic Market. Nobody was hungry, but nobody was fat either—obesity was cured—and absolutely nobody wielded any power. The situation was totally untenable!

Another near miss, this one at half the distance of the previous one, showed us that the gravity inducers hadn't failed—yet—by sending several more personal effects clattering to the deck. I'd had just about enough abuse for one morning, so I flipped open the protective cover on my armrest that hid several switches and thumbed one. An explosion rocked the ship, and stars skewed across the viewer as the force of it sent us spinning. Kik tried to correct and get us back on course, but I thumbed another switch and the starboard main drive cut out.

We could go nowhere now but in circles.

Starships aren't like atmospheric craft; if half your thrust is cut, you can't compensate with the controls. You just spin like one of those whirly firecrackers they light off on the fifth of May, or whenever your local revolutionaries overthrew your local dictatorial government.

Yeah, right...

Well, anyway, the gist of it was that all we had for locomotion now was maneuvering thrusters, atmospheric jets—useless in space—and a can of Jiffy Whip™ that I was saving for emergencies. We were dead in space—well, not literally, but we couldn't move—and the Farfnian cruiser was closing in fast.

The pilot's control couch opened with a sound like parting Velcro®, and Kik shouted, "Damn! Drive's out!" before stepping out and reaching for her jumper.

I fumbled the access hatch to my secret switches closed before she could see them, and managed not to stare at her. Well, okay, so she's a xenophile, but she's also got an awesome and quite female figure, so it's hard not to gape a little when she's getting out of the couch. Did I mention that pilots can't wear clothes with the sensor net on? No? Well, you get the picture. Kik is very striking, despite the fact that she hasn't a hair from her scalp to her toes—one of the fringe benefits of being a pilot—and the lack of eyebrows and even eyelashes makes her face look a little flat.

Well, okay, so I stared a little.

"Overheat on the starboard side," I explained, as if I hadn't caused the whole thing. At times like this I find it easier not to tell the *whole* truth to my crew. They just wouldn't understand. "I don't think anything's blown permanently, but it'll take Zook a while to fix it." I knew better, but as I said, too much information can confuse things sometimes.

"That's assuming they don't just impound the ship and throw us all in the bio-cycler!" Kik sealed the last seam of her jumper, freeing up my eyes for other tasks.

Well, okay, so I stared a lot.

"Well, they're not gettin' me without a fight!" Turk lurched from his seat—an impressive sight since he masses at least twice what I do—and leapt to the weapons locker. I said the ship wasn't armed, not us.

"Let's just see how belligerent they want to be before we lock and load, huh, Turk?" I was trying for my best diplomatic tone, but probably came off as sarcastic, if the muzzle of the small ion cannon pointed at my nose was any indication. I grinned my best please-return-to-your-seats-place-your-seat-backs-and-tray-tables-in-their-full-and-upright-positions-and-don't-vaporize-your-captain grin and opened the communications link that had been blinking for my attention since before the attack.

As our adversaries' faces materialized on the viewer—three very ugly, at least to me, and irate Farfnian faces—I dialed my best angry-lawyer face and let them have both barrels.

"You have damaged this ship and endangered the lives of all those aboard, I'll have you know! I've got full recordings of your unprovoked attack, and I will beam them to the authorities if you don't cease hostilities!"

"We *are* the authorities, as you well know, Captain Harold Eugene Fische."

Boy, he was really torqued! You can always tell when a Farfnian's mad: his mandibles clack together when he speaks, and he uses the longest version of your name he can manage. Kind of like your mother. Except for the mandible thing.

"You are suspected of transporting contraband of an illegal and narcotic nature through Farfnian space." The whole damned spiral arm is Farfnian space, so that was no surprise. "You will allow our boarding party to search your ship without resistance, or we will blast you to dust!"

"Harold?" Kik said with a raised—oops, no eyebrows—whatever.

"Eugene?" Turk quipped with his usual huge, idiot grin, verifying that today could very easily get worse.

"Narcotics? That's ridiculous!" I was still trying for angry lawyer, but was probably only achieving miffed accountant. "Search all you want, but you're not going to find anything!" I flipped off the viewer—or rather *turned* off the viewer, since giving the Farfnian commander the finger would have undoubtedly killed us all instantly—and pushed myself up out of the crash couch, another term I'm not overly fond of.

"Whaddya think you're doin', Harry?" Turk bellowed, glaring at me and waving his weapon around as if it couldn't blow a hole in the hull. He gets a little tense sometimes, in case you hadn't picked up on that. He can't help it. Delayed Stress Syndrome. Six ex-wives will do that to you. "If they board us, they'll find the stash for sure!"

"And if they don't board us, they'll blow us to slag." I shrugged, looked up at him and said, "I'll let you decide whether you'd rather explain the loss of a shipment or try breathing vacuum for a few minutes, but personally I'd rather be alive and poor than dead and rich." I stopped on my way to the airlock and looked back at Turk. "So put that thing away and paint on a smile."

He didn't shoot me, so I guess he took the hint.

CHAPTER TWO

BOARDED

The airlock cycled with a sound like an elephant on a strict diet of refried beans. Well, okay, so it just went *hissssss*, but I was in a pissy mood and attaching unattractive metaphors to everything I could. It's my only release sometimes.

Anyway, the door opened, and Turk, Kik, and I were staring at five very heavily armed and armored Farfnian marines, and one boarding officer. I'd made Turk put away his ion cannon—thank the nondenominational deity of your choice—and told my crew to look as non-threatening as possible. For me, that was easy; I was so scared that my breakfast was trying to come back for an encore appearance. Turk, unfortunately, would look threatening if you stripped him naked, hog-tied him, and painted him pink. That was a problem. Kik, on the other hand, never looks threatening. I don't know how she manages it, but she achieves the rank of "hottie" in the company of any species we encounter.

Maybe it's her perfume.

Uh-huh.

Consequently, instead of being further annoyed by my security officer's belligerent glare, their collective attention was instantaneously captured by my pilot's intragalactic hottiness.

Damn, I'm glad I took her on as pilot!

"Welcome aboard the *Limburger*, good Farfnians. I'm Captain Fische. This is Commander Turk, my security officer, and Lieutenant Kikira, my pilot."

"We will search this ship, Captain Fische!" the boarding officer snapped—literally...remember the mandibles?—taking a step forward. Well, several steps actually, since they have six legs. His five-squad of storm troopers flanked him precisely, two on each side and one directly behind, each leveling a weapon at me and Turk. I had no idea what the guns were; they looked like a handful of linguini with a muzzle of ziti to me. Kik was evidently immune to their aggression. I guess hottiness has its advantages.

"Of course, sir. Where would you like to start?" I waved my hand in a vague directional indication. "The bridge is this way, my quarters are this way, and engineering is this way." They all glared at me. "I suppose you want to see the main hold."

"Do you take us for fools, Captain Fische?"

"Of course not!" I protested, thinking, *You damned well better be, or my ass is going to be sitting in a cold concrete cell for the rest of my life!*

The Farfnians don't fool around with punishment. If the crime is violent, death is the sentence; if it isn't violent, life in prison will make sure you never do it again. And Farfnian prison planets are legendary for their unpleasantness.

"Then take us to the galley, and be quick about it!"

"The *galley*?" I tried on my best puzzled-menial face. "Why would you—"

"The GALLEY!" it roared, turning an interesting shade of mauve. "AT ONCE!"

"Right this way," I said, waving a hand toward Mishi's domain.

"I must explain about my cook before we get there, good Farfnians," I said, my voice edging toward warning. "He is not a very...uh...friendly person." They didn't comment, or even look at me for that matter, but I felt like I should at least warn them. "In fact, he's downright surly at times." Still no response. "And with all the sharp implements in the galley, he can get a little dangerous."

"Your cook will cooperate with us, or he will be arrested." The boarding officer turned his chitinous visage toward me and clacked, "If he becomes violent, he will be vaporized."

"Oh, I understand, I understand." I wasn't about to try to buck this crab. (Everyone calls Farfnians crabs. Maybe it's the ten appendages. Can't be their good temper.) He was holding all the cards, and he knew it. But I could try to protect my ship, couldn't I?

9

"But if you do have to vaporize him, could you tell your troops to use the lowest setting on their weapons? For your own safety as well as ours?"

There have been instances of ship's reactor cores being breached by Farfnian small-arms fire, through more than a dozen decks and a multi-terawatt containment field. Some captains have been known to mount Farfnian small arms on their hulls for ship-to-ship combat. I just didn't want to die because my cook is a hot-tempered little twit.

In response to this, the boarding officer clacked something to his subordinates and they fiddled with their linguini. I hoped they had tweaked the right noodles, and we continued on to the galley.

They pushed through the hatch like they owned the place—which I'm sure they *would* very shortly if they found what they were looking for—and waved their weapons at the array of pots, pans and utensils strewn about the floor from the shockwaves of their earlier barrage. Mishi was nowhere in sight, a fact for which I was duly grateful, but something was cooking. There was a fifty-quart pot on the stove, steam wafting from under the loosely fitting lid.

Officer Crab clacked something to his mates and they fanned out, pointing their weapons at this and that, making sure the place was safe, no doubt, as officers of the law are wont to do in situations like this. Why, a marauding toaster could have leapt out of one of the cabinets and toasted one of them to death! Finally convinced that there were no ambushers in the utensil drawers, they focused their attention on the one appliance they had come to search.

"Not the refrigerator!" Turk squeaked in a whisper next to my ear. "They're gonna find it!"

"Stash it!" I hissed back, keeping my grin in place. I repitched my voice to be heard by the goon squad. "If you tell me what you're looking for..."

"Looking for!" a high-pitched voice screamed from the general direction of the stove.

The pot on the stove rattled until its lid fell off, and five fusion-powered linguini blasters were instantly trained on it.

"Oh crap." Sometimes I'm so eloquent that I astound myself.

"Who the hell is searching *my* galley?"

And with that screeching query, a two-foot-tall, bright-red-skinned little hodgepodge of patched-together oompa-loompa parts lunged up out of the boiling water and landed on the sizzling grill top. Water hissed beneath his four little feet, which were immune to the scalding temperature. Mishi is a Turpenoid, and any temperature below that of boiling water is positively frigid to his caustic little metabolism. He usually sleeps in the oven, though now and then he enjoys a soothing bath. Unfortunately, his temper matches his body temperature. But he's a pretty good cook, anyway.

"Now Mishi, these nice Farfnians are just looking for something. They're not going to disturb your galley."

"Stuff a rat in that hole, Fische!" Mishi bounded off the stovetop and landed at the feet of the boarding officer, glaring up at the chitinous cretin with death in his beady little multifaceted eyes, all four fists on his lumpy little hips. "Get these crabs out of my galley before I boil 'em up for dinner!"

"Silence, Turpenoid, or I will exile you to an ice planet!"

Mishi shut up, which amazed me to no end. I'd never thought to threaten the little imp with cold! Maybe I'm not so smart after all. Well, I was about to find out.

"Open that refrigerator!" the boarding officer clattered, drool escaping its mandibles.

"Why, of course!" I smiled benignly, stepped over my cook—nearly scalding some very tender parts of my anatomy, mind you—and opened the reefer.

"Ah hah!"

"Ah hah?" I asked, looking in at the week-old potato salad, slimy lunchmeat, half a rotten cantaloupe, and a head of romaine lettuce that could probably score higher on a calculus exam than anyone in the room.

"What is that?"

"What?"

"That!" The boarding officer pointed toward a row of paper-thin, neatly stacked yellow squares, each wrapped in its own little cellophane blanket.

"Oh, that. That's for omelets."

"That's contraband!"

"No, it's Crap Shingles®." I shrugged.

"It is narcotic contraband. Individually wrapped wafers of Earth-bovine-species lactational secretions treated with highly toxic Earth-species bacterial colonies! Highly narcotic, addictive, and against the law to possess, sell or distribute within Farfnian space!" It reached one four-fingered lobster hand into the reefer and plucked out a packet. "This is CHEESE!!"

"This is *not* cheese, good Farfnian!" I assured the officer. "This is *simulated* cheese, for consumption by the crew as food." I took a packet out of the reefer and peeled its skin back. "This is just a bunch of chemicals plopped together to *taste* like cheese, I assure you. Look." I flapped the little treasure under his eyestalks until they were weaving back and forth in time to the beat, then I popped it into my mouth, chewed and swallowed with distaste. "It's *fake* cheese."

A stream of spittle dripped from the corner of the boarding officer's mouth, pooling on the floor in a nasty little green puddle.

I had him.

"We will confiscate this contraband for laboratory analysis!" he snapped wetly, spraying spittle in a two-hundred-and-seventy-degree arc.

"Well, if you're going to take that, you'd better take this, too." I reached into a cupboard and pulled out several yellow cardboard bricks about a foot long and three inches square. "We were saving this for chile con queso, but I don't want to get into any more trouble."

"MORE CONTRABAND!!" the boarding officer gabbled, falling over himself to snatch the brick of Velveeta® from my hand.

"No. That's not cheese either, see." I pointed to the plain lettering on the package. "Processed cheese food," I read. "Not real cheese. But if you want to take it, we can eat our chips plain."

"Yes! This, too, we must confiscate!" The boarding officer

waved his troops forward, and each shoveled the packets and bricks of synthetic cheese into their satchels, dumping a plethora of military gear to make room for the booty. "We will...test this contraband for cheese content. If the results come back negative, you will be free to go. Come on!"

The boarding party left the galley at a run, dropping more gear in their wake. Turk picked up one of the linguini blasters and eyed it professionally.

"Careful with that, Turk," I said, making for the corridor. "Let's get back to the bridge."

"Hey, Fische!" Mishi snapped, throwing a spoon at me. It could have been a knife; maybe my luck was changing. "Who's gonna clean up this mess?"

"You are, Mishi, or I'll lock you in the reefer!"

He shut right up.

Life is good.

We arrived on the bridge in time to hear the comm system bleep for our attention. I fell into my chair—Yeah, *chair*. And stop interrupting me. I told you I didn't like that other name for it—and keyed the screen on.

"This is Captain Fische." I looked up into the decidedly bleary eyes—all six of them—of the captain of the Farfnian cruiser.

"Weeee hahfhh teessstted the congr...contrev..." He shook his head, and bits of green and yellow spittle splattered the video pickup; he'd obviously been testing the contraband personally. His eyes focused for a moment. "We found no cheese in the cheese my boarding officer found on your ship, Captain Fische. Please refrain from transporting cheese-like products. You may avoid trouble that way in the future." He waved his mandibles in a Farfnian dismissal. "You are free to go." As the signal faded, I saw a little yellow square being lifted to that crabby face by a wavering lobster hand.

"Well, I guess that *could* have gone worse." Turk dropped into his chair and eyed his new gun. "We got some new toys, anyway."

"Personally, I don't think it could have gone much *better*!" I stretched back in my seat, put my feet up, and sighed.

"What?" Kik glared at me, but, like I said, she couldn't look very scary. "We lost the stash and this trip's going to cost us thousands! We won't be able to afford fuel for the next run!"

"Just get us out of here, Kik, while I scan us for bugs." I flipped a few switches that turned on the ships internal scanners. If the Farfnians had been cognizant enough to leave a tracking or listening device, it would register here.

"You mean back to Earth?" she asked, moving to the pilot's couch and unzipping her jumper.

"Uh..." I pried my eyeballs away and checked my scanner... Negative. Perfect. "No, Kik. Take us to the Carpoolian system. We've got a deal to make."

"With what?" Turk growled, pointing his linguini at me. "The stash is gone!"

"You think we were selling that crap?" I snorted a little laugh of superior intellect. Oh yeah, life is *real* good. "That *was* for sandwiches and omelets, at least if we didn't get boarded." They stared at me in shock, so I thought I'd better explain.

"There are two tons of high-quality Wisconsin cheddar wrapped in static-repulsive monolayer sheeting, buried in an ammonia bath, which is sealed in high-density polycarbonate vacuum crates in the secret hold, behind five hundred cases of rotting sardines. Disgusting, I know, but it throws off the sniffers. It's worth ten-thousand times what those four cases of Crap Shingles® were worth on the cheese market. You still wanna go home?"

"Nope." Kik grinned, dropped her clothes and hopped into the pilot's couch. "Oh, but what about the drive? Can Zook—"

"That Zook's amazing!" I said, thumbing the switch that would make the fake malfunction go away. "He's already fixed it!"

Kik just grinned and closed the hatch. The drive slammed on, pushing us all back in our seats.

"Won't that cruiser get suspicious, Harry?" Turk thumbed a few of his own switches, checking for pursuit.

"Oh, they're all pretty wasted, Turk. I wouldn't worry about them for a week or so." I kicked back, picked out some *good* music and started it spinning. "There are so many weird chemicals in that stuff that those Farfnians are going to have headaches for a month!"

CHAPTER THREE

THE SCORE

If you took a cockroach, crossed it with an octopus, blew it up to something about man-sized, mated it with an attorney, and threw the result into a Vegimatic® on high, you'd probably end up with something that looked, thought, and smelled like a Carpoolian. They are without a doubt the slimiest, most disgusting, most thoroughly loathsome creatures spawned in or out of any ocean in the galaxy. They eat things that would kill a vulture, have the decency of street rats, and can only be considered sentient due to the fact that the first civilized concept their species discovered was currency. If there is one universal constant that is more irrevocable than F=ma, it is that a Carpoolian will do *anything* for money.

You gotta love that.

Hopping through stringspace into the Carpoolian system is like stepping into a solar system-sized garage sale. There are twelve planets in the system. Four are gas giants orbited by planet-sized moons; all these moons are terraformed—or rather, carpooliformed—and every acre of every habitable scrap of land is covered in junk. There is also what looks like an asteroid belt, but there are no asteroids, only the scrapped and empty hulks of millions of derelict spacecraft. And every bit of it—every nut, bolt, bottle, and can—is catalogued, valued and for sale. If there is a commodity in the galaxy, be it animal, mineral, technological, artistic or organic, it can be bought, sold, rented and appraised here. All deals are final, and transactions are either barter, pay-for-service or cash-up-front.

Cash. That was why we were here. That, and the absolute

surety that there wasn't a Farfnian within a parsec who wasn't bought and paid for.

We landed, if one of Kik's gut-wrenching re-entries can be termed a landing, on the Carpoolian home world in what was supposed to be a city, or had been one at one time. It looked like a giant used-car lot, but bigger. A lot bigger.

Before the Farfnians "liberated" them from their backwater ignorance, the Carpoolians had been a friendly, if somewhat obsessed, race of traders, workers and laborers. Unlike humans, however, who adjusted poorly to being told that everything they'd ever made or built was crap, the Carpoolians fell from grace into degradation in the blink of an eye. Less than a year after the first Farfnian ship arrived, a black-market system of illicit trade had cropped up throughout the spiral arm, all because of the Carpoolians, and all right under the noses of their Farfnian oppressors.

This made them the perfect business associates for our little enterprise.

Cash.

That's what we needed and that was what we were after. The Carpoolians were our middlemen—they weren't *men*, not even close, but "middle-aliens" sounds stupid—our distributors to the galaxy, or, more specifically, to the Farfnian public. They were perfect for us and we were perfect for them. They had the logistical infrastructure firmly in place under the Farfnian radar and tested by a thousand of years of graft; we had the product, the one thing that would deliver our pissant little backwater planet out from under the heel—well, claw, really—of the Farfnians.

Cheese...

That sweet amalgam of cow juice and bugs, lovingly cultured on good old Planet Earth, the only place in the galaxy where it could be made, was our deliverance. I didn't really know if cheese *couldn't* be made off-Earth, but try smuggling a cow off-planet. It would have been hard enough if they weren't illegal, but there was no way any human would let one of our sweet bovine benefactors be stolen away. Not with our current corner on the market.

When the jolt of the landing struts settling onto solid ground reverberated through my backside, I was quite ready for some time ashore. But damn if there wasn't some money to be made first.

"Down and safe!" Kik announced over the dying howl of the atmospheric jets and the main drives.

"Well, one out of two, anyway," I said, trying to watch something, anything, but my pilot donning her flight suit. Damn, failed again! So fire me! Oh, that's right, I'm the captain. Can't be fired. Huh, how about that. It's good to be captain sometimes.

"Whaddya mean, one out of two, Harry?" Turk was getting ready for a small beachhead assault, or so it seemed. He was bolting on pieces of body armor with help from the suit's computer. Connect bolt 24-A through slot 34-J; better than any instruction manual. He was also checking an array of armament, including his newly acquired linguini blaster. I hoped he'd figured out how to work that pile of plasma-powered pasta without blowing us all into the next planetary orbit.

"Uh..." Kik sealed the last of her Velcro™ and my brain began functioning again. "I *mean* that our little business transaction is not exactly going to be very safe, which you well know. The Carpoolians have been nervous lately." I thumbed my switches open and hit two. The first conveyored about a metric ton of rotten sardines from the hold into our waste expulsion tanks; the other opened an intercom line to the whole ship. "Shore party to the loading dock. Cargo handlers to the main hold. Anyone shows up without a gun loses a week's pay."

"Mind if I tag along, Harry?" Kik asked, strapping a sexy little laser pistol onto her hip. Okay, so it was just a standard-issue pistol, but anything strapped to Kik immediately becomes sexy by proximity.

Lucky damn pistol!

"I insist!" I picked up an old-fashioned—antique, actually—chemically propelled slug thrower, my remote control, a pack of unfiltered Camels®—Cancer was cured, remember? No guilt there—and my belt, which not only held up my pants, but secreted enough special equipment to get me out of almost any trouble. "Turk, I don't have to tell you to make sure our asses are covered on this, but try not to vaporize our business associates unless they become hostile, okay?"

"No problem, Harry." His voice was muffled and tinny from under the helmet of his body armor, but it hid his face, so I called it even.

"Fine. Let's go, and let me do the talking."

"Sure, Harry," my bridge crew said in perfect unison.

I glared at them both and headed for the hatch, avoiding the big puddles of sarcasm that were oozing up through the floor grating.

The loading dock is the second biggest part of the *Limburger*, but she's a freighter, albeit a small one, so that's not surprising. Only the hold was bigger, and that was now empty. The decoy load had been moved out by automated conveyor, though the smell lingered. The cargo handlers had pumped off the ammonia, opened the seals, and moved the priceless crates of payload onto the lift. Virtually the whole crew was there, even Mishi, who hefted a large-caliber grenade launcher and wore straps of incendiary rounds across his barrel chest. As we all climbed aboard the lift I said a prayer that the rounds wouldn't be cooked off by the little guy's body heat. Hell, he would go up like a volcano if he sneezed.

"Looks like the gang's all here," I said. That wasn't exactly true; Zook, my engineer, wasn't here, but I hadn't asked him to be. Zook is...well, not very social, not even to Mishi's primordial standards, but he can fix anything, and I kind of owe him, so I don't give him much flack. Besides, Zook had a job to do, and to do it he had to stay where he was. I pushed the button on my remote that would lower me and my thirty heavily armed crew down out of the belly of the *Limburger* and into the thick Carpoolian atmosphere. "Everyone put on your party faces."

Only three of my crew threw up with the first whiff of

Carpoolian air. I managed to hold my breakfast down only because I hadn't eaten any, although yesterday's dinner was definitely trying for runner-up. The experienced crew were wearing filter masks, which saved them from the worst of it, but I had to do the negotiating, and Carpoolians don't like anything that hides the face of the one they were negotiating with. They are ruthless hagglers and take every advantage they can get, including reading your facial expressions with uncanny accuracy.

The lift touched down, and Turk's four security people, all armored and breathing canned air—lucky them—took flanking positions. Turk stayed next to me—lucky me—and flipped a few strands of linguini that set his blaster humming like an overheating fusion reactor, which it may well have been for all I knew.

I smiled, dialing up my best car-salesman face, and stepped off the loading platform to greet our odoriferous business associates.

"Neezl!" I chimed, striding forward to embrace the slimy, tentacle-waving, mandible-clapping, gut-wrenching pile of regurgitated sushi. I tried to ignore the smell, the texture of its skin, the wetness oozing through my clothes, and the four Carpoolian thugs pointing guns at me from either side of my squidgy business associate. I'd have to burn this flight suit, but there was no getting around it. Carpoolian custom demanded bodily contact, so I gritted my teeth and let its oozy, writhing embrace envelop me.

"Captain Fisssche!" it sprayed, showering me with saliva the consistency of mayonnaise that had been in the sun too long. "Ssso good to sssee you!"

"And you, Neezl! How is the brood?" It released me and I stepped back, wiping the worst of the goop from my face.

"Oh, they are ssssliming along nicely, thank you!"

"And how is business?"

"Ahhhh, bussssssinesssss is bad, Harry. The crabsss are all over usss like ssslime on a Carpoolian'sss butt cheeksss." Way too much information there. "But that isss not your concern. We are here to do busssinesssinessss, isss it not ssso?"

"We are indeed, good Neezl." I turned and waved an arm at the laden loading platform. Two of my cargo handlers had liberated a crate of product and placed it upon a folding table. Ten one-kilo bricks of golden-yellow cheddar, worth ten times their weight in actual gold, had been arranged in a neat row for our perusal. Kik was waving one graceful hand over the blocks of cheese in her best game-show-hostess imitation, bless her theatric little heart. "I have brought you treasure beyond your wildest dreams, Neezl: two metric tons of pure Wisconsin cheddar, uncut and unpasteurized. The absolute best!"

"Looksss like processsed cheessse food to me," Neezl said, sliming over to the table. It poked one of the plastic-wrapped bricks with the tip of a tentacle and made a noncommittal noise. "We'll have to tessst it."

"Test away! But I hope your tester's got a strong constitution!" I backed away from the table, knowing what was coming and wanting no part of it.

The best technology in the galaxy had yet to provide a reliable test that would confirm the presence and concentration of the elusive mixture of biochemicals in cheese that provided the intoxicating effect to the Farfnian physiology. Neezl waved a tentacle at one of its thugs, and the creature squidged forward with a small satchel. It handed the satchel to Neezl, who flipped it open and withdrew a small chitinous bundle about the size of a terrestrial rat. The little creature was called a Farfnian mud puppy; at least, that's what we called it. It looked like a small, deformed lobster. *Panulirus argus*, not *Homarus americanus*. Oh, sorry. Don't know lobsters? I mean the ones with no pincers. The Farfnians probably had a different name, but they treated the little things like pests. Their value to the rest of the galaxy was in the one thing they had in common with the sentient species of their home planet; they shared the same physiological mechanism that triggered euphoria from cheese. This was our test subject, and it was going for the ride of its short little life.

Neezl picked one brick of cheese from the ten on the table and waved the others away. When Kik had removed the rest, the Carpoolian placed the mud puppy on the table, and produced a small knife from the folds of its slimy garment. The little lobster-like creature was already sniffing around the table, undoubtedly picking up trace amounts of cheese on its sensitive mandibles. The knife flashed in the withering light, and Kik actually gasped, as if she didn't know exactly what was going on.

The blade missed the mud puppy by a wide margin, of course, but it did nick the plastic skin protecting the one-kilo brick of Wisconsin's finest. The mud puppy's antennae perked up like an alarm klaxon had gone off in its tiny little mind. The little creature clattered over to the golden brick at full speed, its mandibles immediately seeking out the hairline rupture in the plastic skin. The sharp mouthparts sliced into the opening greedily, and the lobsteroid's whole body shivered in glee. It lunged at the plastic-coated brick, slashing through the protective covering in an instant, and burrowed right in. When its tail vanished into the cheese, Neezl raised its slimy brow in surprise.

"Well, thisss appearsss to be quite pure."

The brick of cheese quivered.

"Wait for it," I said, taking another precautionary step back.

The cheese bobbled and jerked, little glimpses of ruddy-red chitin visible as the mud puppy burrowed around in circles, turning every time it hit plastic. It burrowed and ate and ate and burrowed until there was very little cheese left and the plastic covering was becoming tight around its bloated body. Without any more cheese to devour, the hyper-euphoric little alien decided that the residual cheese on the plastic was just too delectable to pass up. It began eating its constricting covering, backing out of the ruptured plastic wrapping as it munched, like a snake shedding its skin in reverse. Finally it lie there, its tiny legs splayed out in all directions, soft interior flesh bulging from between chitinous plates like a hundred-kilo woman in a size-two bikini. It was unable to crawl, but still sniffed about looking for more cheese to devour.

"Asss I sssaid, this appearsss to be—"

The little mud puppy quivered again, coughed once, and exploded.

Bits of mud puppy and partially digested cheese sprayed in a three-hundred-sixty-degree arc, spattering everyone within two meters. Neezl had been watching very closely, but didn't seem to mind the noisome bits of slimy shrapnel that spattered its hide. Kik turned her head and made a face, but I was watching Neezl like a hawk inspecting a mouse. Mud puppies rarely ate more than their own body weight in cheese, and for one to eat to the point of detonation was rare indeed. This was *very* pure cheese.

"Well, Neezl?" I said, moving closer. "What do you think of our product?" What could it think? There was enough high-quality cheese here to hook a planet full of Farfnians, and once hooked, the Carpoolians would be supplying their insatiable appetites with cheese for the rest of their lives. Neezl was going to be embarrassingly rich very soon. "I'll sell you the whole load for fifty thousand per brick." *May as well shoot for the stars*, I thought.

"It isss too pure," it said, blinking its asymmetrical pupils at me blankly.

"*Too* pure?" I blinked back, taken quite aback by its claim. "How can cheese be *too* pure, Neezl? That's like saying money is *too* valuable, or the sex was *too* good, or you are *too* rich!"

"It isss too pure for direct dissstribution, Harry." It backed away and made some odd motion with one tentacle. Its four goons closed in around it like buzzards descending on road kill. "Dissstributing product of thisss potency will drive down the value of every gram of cheessse on the market."

"So step on it a little." I was showing my anger now, waving my arms and raising my voice, not the healthiest practice with such an array of weaponry pointing in both directions. "Blend it with some old crap, or imitation cheese, and sell it as pure. You make twice as much as you would have from twice the volume."

"That cossstsss money, Captain," it said. "I cannot pay that price for thisss product. I will pay twenty-five thoussssand per brick. That isss final." Being demoted from Harry to Captain was a serious blow, and I took it poorly, but having my price cut in half was more than I could take.

Don't get me wrong, I knew that this was all a ploy, a bargaining strategy. Neezl couldn't refute the results of the purity test and it didn't want to pay what the stuff was really worth, so it had to make up something to tip the scales back in its favor.

Too pure, my ass! I thought, gritting my teeth. *Fine, if this spiny little squid wants to play hardball, let's show it some heat!*

"Charley!" I barked to my chief cargo handler without taking my eyes off of the Carpoolians. "Pack it up! We're leaving! Turk! If the Carpoolians so much as twitch a tentacle, make a crater. A big one."

"Aye, Captain!" Turk moved in front of me and I suddenly felt as safe as if I was in my mother's womb. He fiddled with his linguini—that's starting to sound slightly obscene, isn't it?—and pointed the humming weapon at the tight group of Carpoolians.

Several things happened in the span of a few heartbeats.

The cargo handlers started packing up the product, everyone else pointed weapons at someone, and, to my dismay, four heavily armed Carpoolian skimmers swooped over the tops of the buildings surrounding the landing field, their huge ion cannons trained on our tidy little group. My ace had just been trumped.

"You will not leave, Captain Fisssche!" Neezl slurred, sliming out from the tight knot of its thugs. It was unarmed and squidged its way right up in front of Turk's weapon, staring us down fearlessly.

No wonder Carpoolians are so good at this, I thought. *They've either got balls as big as watermelons, or fear is not in their makeup.* I'd bargained with them many times before, and with Neezl more than once, but things had never gone this far.

"Do you intend to *take* this cheese from us, Neezl?" I asked blithely, stepping out to stand beside Turk. "If you do, you'll never sell cheese in this galaxy again, I can tell you that!"

"And who isss to sssay that I do not have other sssuppliersss, Captain?"

"Who, Tillamook? They can't handle the volume! The

French? You know the Farfnians don't like that smelly stuff. Besides, you know as well as I that there are far more distributors than there are suppliers. You're not the only squid in the sea, Neezl!"

"I will pay thirty thousand per brick, and that isss asss high as I can go, Harry."

Oh, so now I'm Harry again? So suddenly? I knew I had it right where I wanted it, but I needed to give as well as I got.

"You'll pay fifty thousand, Neezl, and I'll tell you exactly why." I took a step and showed the Carpoolian the remote I'd been keeping in my pocket. "This controls many of the functions of my ship; I can raise and lower the cargo lift." I demonstrated by raising it a foot and dropping it back down. "I can turn on the flood lights." I demonstrated again. "And I can turn off the containment field on the main reactor core." I thumbed a switch and said, "Ready, Zook?"

"I am most assuredly ready to push the button that will end my eternal pain, whenever you are, Captain," came a tinny voice from my remote.

"You wouldn't." Neezl sounded different. I hoped that difference was fear.

"Why not?" I was getting tired of this.

"Zook wouldn't!" Yep, fear all right.

"Zook's an Immortal, Neezl," I explained, "and he's been feeling a little depressed lately."

Neezl's pupils dilated until blackness engulfed his whole eye. Immortals, in case you didn't know, are very rare. You may have even seen one and not known it, since they change bodies regularly. They're an ancient race, pre-Farfnian by about a hundred-million years or so, and they have unlocked the secret of immortality. The trouble, it seems, with immortality is boredom. They tend to be suicidal, which explains why there are so few of them. Zook likes me because I make his life interesting. He quite literally lives for moments like this.

"You'd rather kill usss all, than fly away with sssixty million farfsss?"

That's the denomination of Farfnian currency, in case you've been living under a rock.

"I was told to bring back a hundred million, and not a farf less. So if I die here, or die later at the hands of my employer, what's the difference to me?" I let him percolate on that a while, then said, "But that doesn't mean I'm not prepared to sweeten the deal a little."

I thumbed another button, and the *Limburger's* waste-expulsion tanks dumped. Usually we do this in space, preferably during reentry so that all the…um…stuff is vaporized. In fact, we'd done so before landing, so the only thing in the tanks was five-hundred cases of quite rotten sardines. It hit the ground with a predictable sound—eeew—and the flimsy cardboard, well-saturated with sardine juice, ruptured on impact. The resulting stench made the Carpoolian atmosphere smell like Channel N° 5®, and two more of my crew lost their breakfast. The Carpoolians, on the other hand, stared at the offal with the gleam of hunger in their eyes and drool dripping from their nasty little mouths.

"Forty," Neezl said flatly.

"Fifty, and a signed contract from Wisconsin Cheese Inc. naming you as our sole distributor for the next year."

"Forty-five and two yearsss. And sssimilar ssshipments of sssuch delicaciesss with every load."

"Fifty and a five-year contract at the same price, barring any variance in product purity, and a personal assurance that future shipments will be encased in much more nasty things than now grace your landing field, Neezl."

"Loan me your pilot for the afternoon and we've got a deal, Captain Fisssche."

My jaw must have dropped; I couldn't explain why my tonsils were getting cold any other way. I closed my mouth, thinking that the flavor of the air was fitting the temper of this deal better with every breath I took.

"I don't trade in *people*, Neezl! Think of something else." Either Kik's reputation had grown since our last trip out, or her intragalactic hottiness was more potent than I thought.

"Captain, I—" I turned to Kik, saw the glint in her eye, and shuddered.

"No, Kik. Not with a Carpoolian."

"Not *that*, Harry!" She shot me a scowl, which isn't easy without eyebrows. "Carpoolians don't do that! They're broadcast spawners. They just find a nice cesspool and—"

"I get the picture, Kik. Thanks!" Double eeeew! I shuddered again, then looked to Neezl and said, "Then why?"

"I am entertaining a client from Sssheessshar thisss afternoon, Harry."

Kik's nails dug into my bicep with enough force to puncture the skin.

"Say *yes*, Harry," she whispered in my ear.

I knew about Sheesharians. Everyone did. Hell, *I* might even bend the rules if I were propositioned by one. They were the most beautiful, ethereal creatures in the galaxy, and their whole philosophy of life was empathy. When they touch you, they feel whatever you feel, so the better you feel, the better they feel, and they were reputedly very good at making almost any sentient species feel very, very good. I could feel Kik's hand trembling through the tortured nerves in my arm.

"Done," I said.

Everyone whooped in delight. Hands shook tentacles. The skimmers shipped their weapons, swooped down and started disgorging sealed crates of money. My security troops moved out of the way, and the cargo handlers started moving cheese onto one of the skimmers. I didn't notice any of it because Kik was hugging me, her lips pressed to my neck just below my ear as she whispered, "Thank you, thank you, thank you."

Oh, yeah. Sometimes I like my job a lot.

Lucky damn Sheesharian.

CHAPTER FOUR

A NIGHT ON THE TOWN

"Lucky damn Sheesharian," I muttered, downing the rest of my Glenfiddich™ and crushing out my cigarette.

The deal was done.

The money was onboard and well-hidden, the ship was secure, the core was rigged to blow if anyone broke in, and captain and crew were enjoying some well-deserved R&R. The Carpoolians may stink, but they do business with almost every sentient, and many not-so-sentient, species in the galaxy. Their entertainment facilities were wide-ranging, and the tidy little pub in which I was currently drinking didn't even smell bad. The place even had a human bartender. At least, she looked human. It's hard to tell sometimes, you know. I heard laughter from down the bar and turned to see Turk trying to win a bet by drinking a yard of ale without using his hands. He was winning, but wet.

So why wasn't I having fun?

"Refill, Harry?"

"Sure." I squinted at the bartender as she poured. *Human*, I decided, *or close enough.* "What's your name again?"

"Laila." She finished topping off my drink and nodded to the impatient patron down the bar. "Right there, hon."

I glared down the bar, and the guy put his hand down. He had to; I was his boss. In fact, most of the crew was here. We'd all piled into one of the Carpoolian's vehicles—yeah, okay, there's a joke there, but I'm ignoring it—and they drove us to the best human joint in the district. The result was one impromptu party. I pulled another cigarette from my dwindling pack and held the end against Mishi's head long enough to start it smoldering.

"Thanks, Mish," I mumbled, patting his multi-layered thermal overcoat and almost singeing my hand.

"Huh?" He looked at my lit smoke and grinned. "Oh, don't mention it! Another Flaming Garbanzo over here, Sweet Cheeks!"

"Sure." Laila pulled a bottle of two-hundred-proof alcohol off the rack and poured a shot, then took a book of matches and snipped the heads off the whole pack, letting them drop into the drink. She lit the top with a silver Zippo™ and said, "There you go, Pepper Puss."

Mishi downed the drink without putting out the flame. There was a muffled explosion and smoke trailed from his nostrils.

"Aaaaahhhhh. Good stuff!"

"So what's a beautiful girl like you doing in a dump like this?" I asked Laila, sipping my scotch. I'd never heard that one before! Honest!

"It pays the bills," she came back without batting an eye. They were nice eyes, I decided, and the rest of her wasn't bad either. "How about I just leave this here and go see about some of the other customers?"

She placed the half-empty—damn straight, I'm a pessimist—bottle before me and strolled down the bar. I watched her go, deciding that her eyes maybe weren't her best feature after all.

"I understand that drowning is supposed to be a very euphoric experience."

"Huh?" I looked at Zook, his comment having caught me totally flatfooted.

"Drowning. You know. Death by asphyxiation while submerged in water."

"I know what drowning is, Zook." I peered into his nut-brown face, those dark eyes, the pearly white teeth. He looked to all the world like a human, mid-thirties maybe, black hair, sub-Asian or Middle Eastern ancestry. I knew otherwise. He was more alien than any *thing* I'd ever met. An immortal with a death wish... Jeez, how pathetic can you get?

"Yes, well, I have read that the experience of drowning is very euphoric. I have been thinking of—"

"No, Zook. Not drowning. It's no good." I took a deep drag and blew smoke over my shoulder at Mishi. Smoke keeps the little fireplug in a good mood.

"Why is drowning being no good, Harry?"

"Too wet," I said, declining to elaborate.

Talking Zook out of offing himself was a full-time job. Sometimes I thought I'd just let him do it if he weren't such a good engineer. Well, Zook wasn't actually an engineer *per se*, but Immortals have about a hundred-million-year head start on cutting-edge technology, so anything we humans, or even the Farfnians, can cook up is pretty simple by their standards. I'd asked him to upgrade the *Limburger* about a million times, but he'd only said, "No, Harry. That wouldn't be fair."

When I eventually asked him who it wouldn't be fair to, he said, "Why, the *Limburger*, of course."

Whatever. Subject dropped. Damn Immortals.

"Too wet..." Zook's shoulders slumped. He stared into his untouched beer and heaved a deep sigh.

Pathetic.

"Hey, Zookie! How about immolation!" Mishi swiveled around on his bar stool and blew a smoke ring at the depressed Immortal.

"Immolation?" One of Zook's dark eyebrows arched speculatively.

"Yeah, you know, find a nice flammable liquid; plenty available right here." He waved his hand and almost caught my scotch on fire. I rescued it and glared at him, but he didn't take the hint. "You dump about a gallon over your head, light a match, and FOOSH!" He threw up all four arms and almost fell off his barstool. I considered giving him a nudge to help.

"Immolation, huh?" Zook raised his other eyebrow and pouted his lower lip in thought. "Well, I would certainly be—"

"No, Zook. Not immolation. It's no good," I said, finishing my drink and pouring myself another.

"Why is immolation being no good, Harry?"

"Too hot."

"Too hot..." His shoulders slumped again.

Pathetic.

"Hey! What's that! Turn that up!" someone yelled from down the bar.

I looked up at the media sphere. A Carpoolian anchor-squid was flailing all of its tentacles in front of a three-dee schematic of blinking arrows surrounding a sphere. I was off my barstool—no, I didn't *fall* off, smartass—before Laila even touched the volume.

"I repeat!" the Carpoolian voice blared, "A fleet of Farfnian war cruisers has fallen out of stringspace to surround every inhabited planet in the system. All independent business interests are advised to see to your property. Foreign extracarpoolians are advised to return to your ships or report to your embassies."

"Crap!" That's me, Mister Eloquent-Under-Pressure. "Back to the *Limburger*!" I shouted over the noise. "Grab any transport you can! Zook, you're with me! Mishi, you, too! Come on!"

"Look!" someone else shouted.

I looked. The picture said it all. It was a telescopic view of one of the huge Farfnian battleships, and it was hurtling an asteroid roughly the size of my ship at the planet below. This planet. They were dropping rocks. Big rocks.

"Double crap!"

The whole bar suddenly shook like a giant pit bull was very angry with it. That was amazing, considering that we were twelve floors underground. Several people fell, several more screamed, some did both.

"Come *on*!" I grabbed Zook, who was staring up at the cracks that had begun to spider web the ceiling, and pushed him toward the stairs. It would be a long climb, but better than getting trapped in the elevator. "Everybody out!"

Everyone rushed for the exits, except for Laila.

"Come on!" I grabbed her arm, but she jerked free, shaking her head.

"I can't leave!" she screamed.

"Sure you can! You're off duty. That's automatic during alien invasions!"

30

"No, I can't!"

I was about to ask why when she showed me. She pulled back her lapel and showed me the red triple-crescent tattoo that explained everything.

Laila wasn't real. She was a clone, and by definition, clones weren't people, they were property.

"Triple crap!" I yelled, grabbing her wrist. "I'm buying you! Right now! I'll mail your owner a freaking money-o-gram!"

We made it to the stairs before the ceiling collapsed.

The climb to the surface was as miserable and dusty as you can probably imagine. Having a beautiful clone hold my hand all the way up made it less miserable, but no less dusty. In case you hadn't noticed, I tend to take any perk I can get.

When we got to the surface, however, things really started to look bleak. I squinted through the dusty air at the horizon to the east, where three immense mushroom clouds blotted out the sky. One was fairly close, and undoubtedly accounted for the shockwave that had collapsed the bar. To the west I could see the contrails of two down-bound asteroids. Things were going to hell very quickly.

"We need transport!" I screamed to Zook.

"I'll see what I can find!" He ran off through the debris-littered streets, grinning like an idiot. The bastard was enjoying himself.

"The rest of the crew took all the cars!" Mishi squawked, flapping his arms in four-fisted frustration. "The ingrates took all the transport, and they'll probably take the ship!"

"Nope!" I said, sifting through my pockets. I pulled out the keys and jingled them in front of his face by the little rabbit's foot that I hoped was working, though I had my doubts. "Not without these, they're not."

"So now all we gotta do is get there!" I hadn't improved the Turpenoid's temper with my assurance at all, and he looked about ready to boil over.

MEEP-MEEP!

We turned toward the sound, and for the second time that day my tonsils got some air-conditioning.

"You're freakin' kidding me!" Mishi sputtered, glaring at Zook as he zoomed up on a brand-new, shiny Scoot-Air™ S-137.7 sky scooter.

Just in case you didn't know, 137.7 is the maximum carrying capacity in kilos of the tiny, one-passenger vehicle. I would have said, "Quadruple crap," but my vocal cords and brain weren't on speaking terms.

"There's *four* of us, you imbecilic, immortal, im-compoop!"

Sometimes I wish I were as eloquent as Mishi in situations like this. Zook just grinned.

"I souped it up a little. It'll fly us." He pointed toward the east. "And from the look of things, we had better get aboard, although it would be a most interesting way to—"

"Shut up, Zook!" Good vocal cords... Good brain... Friends again? "Mishi, get on the handle bars. I'll drive. You two stand on the running boards and hang on to me!"

We did that, and I'll be boiled in cheese dip if, when I pushed the riser pedal, the little scooter didn't take right off. Just in time for the shockwave of the nearest asteroid impact to almost knock us out of the air.

I twisted the throttle until I thought it would break off in my hand, but it didn't, and we shot toward the spaceport like a bullet from a gun. Mishi and Laila managed to hit exactly the same note—high E-flat, I think—but we didn't hit anything, including the ground. Zook grinned and shouted something about how long it had been since he'd had this much fun. I don't remember much. I was too busy staying alive.

Needless to say, we made it to the ship; I wouldn't be telling you this if we hadn't. We landed in a screeching, screaming, laughing—damn Immortal—pile, and got disentangled with only minor burns—damn Turpenoid. The rest of the crew was glaring at us, having discovered that the door was locked.

"Sorry we're late, but someone took all the big cars." I pulled my keys out and pushed a button. The ship went *chirp-chirp*, and the loading platform lowered. We all piled on. I was giving orders on the way up.

"Zook, I need the mains online yesterday. Turk, you're on tactical; I need a readout on every ship in orbit if we're going to get out of here. Everyone else, get strapped down. It's going to be a rough ride when Kik flies us through—"

My heart stopped.

I know my heart stopped, because I was listening to it. Problem was, it started up again.

"Kik..." I said numbly, brain and vocal cords struggling to stay happy together.

"Crap!" Turk said.

I had to agree.

We had no pilot.

CHAPTER FIVE

PILOT, PILOT, WHO'S GOT MY PILOT?

I looked at Laila. "I don't suppose you can pilot a stringship."

"I can't even drive a car!" Her voice was edged with hysteria, but then so was mine.

"What the hell are we gonna do, Harry!?" Turk was so pale that I thought he might have made a mistake in his body armor. "We're freakin' *stuck* here!"

"I suppose that being crushed by a falling asteroid would be an interesting way to—"

"Shut *up*, Zook!" I swallowed, thinking hard. I knew I was thinking hard because my scalp started feeling warm. That happens to me sometimes.

"Turk, you, Mishi, Laila and Zook come with me to the bridge! Everyone else, man your stations. Things are going to get rough."

"Me?" Mishi and Zook spouted in perfect unison. The rest of the crew started to stumble off. Some of them were stumbling because they were scared, some because the ground was shaking, and some because they were drunk. I'd had a few drinks myself, but I don't get much of a buzz from alcohol. More is the pity; I could have used a stiff drink!

"I need both of you if we're going to survive this! Come on!"

"But who's going to pilot this thing?" Either the Carpoolian atmosphere was leaking into the ship, or I was right about my assessment of the interior of Turk's body armor. I hoped none of the electronics shorted out.

"I am," I told them. It was nice to see other people's tonsils getting some air for a change.

"But you're not a pilot, Harry!"

"No," I admitted as we all piled into the lift that would take us to the bridge deck, "but I will be when Zook gets finished wiring the ship's computer into my brain."

"That sounds like fun." If there's anything I hate more than a pathetic, suicidal immortal, it's a smug, pathetic, suicidal immortal.

"When he *what?*" Turk grabbed my arm, and very nearly wrenched it right out of the socket. His face was so red that I thought his head would explode, so I figured that I'd better explain. As I did, he seemed to calm down. Either that, or he had an aneurysm and was brain dead—or brain deader, rather.

Remember I mentioned earlier that I had a prosthetic? One of those new high-tech ones? Well, mine is slightly more high-tech than most. I acquired it my first trip out. I was just a mule then, traveling on a commercial liner, my stomach full of cheese-filled plastic pouches—and yes, it is a thoroughly disgusting procedure to retrieve those little packages. The short story: I was caught by a Farfnian customs inspector while checking my bags through spaceport security and I was stupid enough to run. The rotten crab shot me right in the back of the head. Thankfully, the gun he used was supposed to only incapacitate the target. Unthankfully, the little dart penetrated my skull and started paralyzing my brain. I would have been dead inside half an hour if not for Zook.

I hadn't known at the time that the irritating little fellow seated next to me on the liner, the one who'd bored me to tears through three star systems, was an Immortal. I don't know exactly what happened—I was a little unconscious at the time—but when the crowd cleared and the Farfnian official tried to claim his prize, my body was gone. Zook had scooped me up and dragged me off to some dark corner, where he did something that I'd have never thought possible.

He downloaded my brain onto his palm computer.

As I said, Immortals' technology makes the rest of us look like we're still scraping rocks together hoping for a spark. Their computers are amazing, and they all carry around small units that are made to interface with *any* mainframe and download everything. Well, evidently the human brain is no more than a rather simple computer, and after he'd downloaded Harry Fische onto his palm-sized miracle, he simply plucked out the pesky little dart that would have killed me, performed a little brain surgery, slid his computer in between the two hemispheres of my—now dead—brain, and let it take over.

I woke up with a headache hearing computer voices, which is why I hate them so much.

But I'm better at math now.

No surprise there.

Suffice to say that I like Zook, even if he is pathetic. I've been talking him out of killing himself ever since, along with trying to find something to capture his interest. Maybe wiring me to the ship's computer would keep him occupied for a while.

"But why wire you to the *Limburger*, Harry?" Zook is a brilliant technician, don't get me wrong, but he doesn't really think things through sometimes.

"I can't pilot and find Kik at the same time, Zook. I need to fly, use the sensors, communicate, and receive tactical information from Turk. I can't do all that without being hardwired in."

"And me?" Mishi asked, glaring up at me. "I'm freezing my patootie off up here! Why can't I go hide in the oven?"

"I'll need you to do the soldering, and maybe some cauterizing," Zook said, finally thinking ahead. I was proud of him.

"And what about me?" Laila was more than a little scared, but she'd have been dead if she hadn't come with us, so I guess she figured every minute was a plus. "Why am I here?"

"Moral support," I said with my best dashing-space-captain smile.

"Harry, I've got two skills: I mix drinks and (**expletive deleted**)." She stared at me and I stared back. We both blinked. "If you're using *me* for moral support, we're in deep trouble!"

"We're in deep trouble," I said.

"Deep trouble," Zook agreed.

"Very deep," Turk said with a nod.

"Deeper than (expletive deleted) in a septic tank, Baby." Okay, sometimes Mishi is a little *too* eloquent.

"Besides," I told her with a smile as the lift opened and we all entered the bridge, "you have to sit in my chair and talk to the Carpoolians."

"Me?" Her voice had raised two octaves...very cute.

"Yep, you! You just got promoted to Intragalactic Liaison Officer." I waved a hand at my chair. "Have a seat, and don't touch any of the switches hidden under the armrests, okay?"

"Uh, sure." She sat very carefully, a little stunned, I think. Evidently being freed from a lifetime of slavery, saved from a collapsing bar ceiling, *and* landing a job on a cheese-running stringship was too much for her to handle in one single day.

"Let's do this, Zook!"

"Right away, Harry," he said with a grin, opening up his tool kit.

I won't describe the next five minutes simply because I didn't see or feel very much. I just sat on the edge of the pilot's couch and relaxed while several hair-thin wires were tunneled through my skull and into my—albeit prosthetic—brain. The next thing I knew, I felt something click in my head, and I could think inside the *Limburger's* computer.

Very cool!

"That's it! You're wired, Harry."

"Thanks, Zook," I said, trying to ignore the smell of burnt hair, skin, and solder. "You, too, Mish. You can go hide in the oven now."

"Thanks, Harry." He trundled out, headed toward warmer climes.

"You stay here, Zook. I may need some help before we're out of this."

"Sure, Harry!" He *was* having fun. Well, good for him, if not for the rest of us.

I opened the pilot's couch and looked inside at the sticky membranous interior. I took a deep breath, peeled out of my jumpsuit and climbed in—ick, ick, double ick. The lid closed and enveloped me in slimy, sticky, neuro-conducting membrane—triple ick. Then, about a billion molecular fibers tunneled into my skin, eyes, ears, nose and every other orifice—*ick!*—and I suddenly understood why Kik loved being a pilot so much.

All at once, I *was* the *Limburger*.

I could feel the ship, the power, the engines; I could see all around us at once, the ship's sensory data being interpreted by my eyes as images I could understand. There was nothing between me and the outside world, and with my new link to the computer, I could talk to my crew, give orders, and even see *inside* myself—or the ship, rather. This was going to be something else!

"We're taking off, Turk. Make sure everybody's strapped down. It might get bumpy."

I fired up the drives and atmospheric jets, and felt the power...

Effing-A, was all I could think as we leapt off the ground and thundered at low altitude over the city.

"Laila!" I said, using my computer link to open up a communications channel to Neezl. "Find out where this Carpoolian has taken Kik. She's supposed to be entertaining a...uh...client of theirs."

"Uh, okay, Harry."

I would have watched her conversation, but I was a little busy. Aside from the city being pummeled by asteroids, ships were taking off from everywhere, some from areas of the city where there were no facilities to handle them. I was dodging more than I was flying, but we hadn't hit anything yet, and we were making good time even if it *was* rush hour.

"There's an incoming, Harry!" Turk was a little calmer now, and evidently hadn't blown out an artery in his brain. "North-northeast. Looks like impact about ten klicks out."

"I see it," I told him. "We should be past the worst of it when it hits."

"Lot of ships taking off, Harry," he said.

"How many?"

"Dunno. Thousands, if you believe the sensors. The Farfnians have about fifty ships in-system. They're outnumbered by a lot, but a lot of outbound ships have taken hits. Most are running. It's a mess up there."

"Good! We'll be able to slip through. Now where—"

"I found her, Harry!" Laila announced, her voice much more steady. Well, maybe she had some chutzpa after all. "She's in some kind of an embassy building. Neezl gave me the address."

"Open the left armrest of my chair, Laila." I watched her do so. "Now type in the address on that keypad. Good!"

It was in my brain, bearing and distance calculated automatically by the computer. Kik was right; this was better than sex. But then, how would I know? It's been a while.

I hammered the main drives and cringed as a couple of buildings melted behind us. It probably would have been safer if I'd gained some altitude, but I didn't have the time. Turk kept up a constant update of the tactical situation, and things were quickly turning into a very sticky situation. I banked the ship around a very tall building that was teetering with the shockwaves of recent asteroid impacts, and wondered just what the hell the Farfnians thought they were doing.

Surely they weren't annihilating a whole solar system just to cut off the cheese market! That was taking the War on Cheese a bit too far. Rather like spanking a naughty child with a broadsword, I would think.

Finally, the embassy came into visual sensor range.

"Crap! There's no place to land!"

"Huh?" That was Turk, in his usual Einsteinian manner.

"There's no freaking room to park the freaking ship!" Okay, I was a little miffed. "The streets are too narrow!"

"Land on top, Harry."

"What?" I ran some numbers through the ship's computer and got the same answer as the one from the computer in my head. It just took longer. "You're crazy, Zook! It won't hold us!"

"Not if you just drop the ship on the building, Harry. Touch down and leave the atmospheric lifters on station-keeping. We won't crush it. Well, not very badly anyway."

"Fine." I brought the ship in over the building and let her settle down *slowly* onto the roof. "Get ready, Turk, and get me a gun! I'm going with you and we don't have time to negotiate!" I heard his reply—far too gleeful for my taste—just as the landing struts touched the roof and punched right through the top two floors. I set the lifters, the belly of the ship resting like a five-hundred-ton feather on top of the embassy building, and ordered the pilot's couch to open.

The neuro-conducting membrane peeled away from me and I struggled up out of the couch, unplugging the thin wires from the back of my head with a cringe.

"Harry?" I looked to Laila as I reached for my jumpsuit, realizing that I was buck naked, but in too much of a hurry for modesty.

The look on her face stopped me in my tracks.

Her eyes were wide and roamed from my head to my toes and back up. Her hand was in front of her mouth, hiding a smile.

"Oh, Harry!" Then she laughed out loud.

I am not what you would call a vain man, mind you, but when a pretty woman looks at you *sans* clothing and *laughs*, it does something bad to your soul. My face must have fallen about a meter before Turk interrupted my misery.

"Not any more, he's not."

Laughter broke out across the bridge, all three of them, staring at me and giggling helplessly. I couldn't stand it. Then a thought crossed my mind, and I looked down.

Oops, no hair. Damn. Hadn't thought about that. And with a name like mine... Irony can be so cruel sometimes.

I chose to believe that my lack of hair was the *only* reason for my bridge crew's mirth, propped my damaged ego back into place, and quickly donned my jumpsuit.

"Harry, I'm sorry, but I—"

"Forget it," I told Laila. "Occupational hazard of all pilots. Now you know why I'm *captain*." I tried to put a little emphasis on the last word, and maybe it worked, or maybe they only stopped laughing because I was dressed. But my head was still as slick as a cue ball, so maybe it was the emphasis after all. Yeah. Uh-huh. The emphasis, for sure.

"Let's go, Turk!"

"Aye aye, Captain!"

He handed me a gun. It was some kind of rifle thingy, with a little flat-screen sight that had red arrows that pointed at the target and said, "Kill this?" It was the idiot-proof version, I guess. Good thing. Sometimes I think my crew knows me too well.

"Keep the motor running, Zook. We'll be right back!"

Turk, four of his security men, and I left the ship and entered the building through a hole that was left after Turk fired his linguini blaster at a heavily armored door. Laila had told us where exactly to find Kik, but there were a lot of hallways, doors and screaming, twittering, sliming, and squidging aliens all trying to evade us, one another, and their impending dooms. I suppose that landing a ship on the roof hadn't improved matters, but there was nothing I could do about that.

One particularly stupid creature pointed a weapon at us and slavered something that sounded angry. I didn't get a good look at it, and after Turk and his crew fired, there wasn't much left to examine. I hoped he wasn't important.

"This is it!" Turk shouted, leveling his cannon at a small ornate door.

"Whoa! Hold on there, Turk!" I gently prodded the muzzle of his weapon until it pointed aside. "Kik could be standing right on the other side, eh? Let's try the subtle approach."

"Fine."

He raised one huge armored boot and kicked the door. It flew right off the frame and clattered to the floor, only slightly less damaged than if he'd blasted it with his cannon. I looked at him and sighed.

"Actually, Turk, I was thinking about knocking."

"Knocking?" He said it like the word meant nothing to him. Maybe it didn't. I didn't have time to explain.

"Forget it." I stepped through the door, and stopped.

I will not describe what I saw.

I remember it quite well, but I will not relate it to you.

In fact, I wish I could forget what I saw, but it will forever be indelibly imprinted in my prosthetic brain. Maybe I can get Zook to delete it someday.

Suffice to say, we found Kik.

We also found the Shesharrian ambassador.

They were busy.

I felt obligated to interrupt, but didn't know exactly how to do so. If Turk kicking in their door hadn't distracted them from their...uh...busy-ness, my stern "Ah-hem!" was certainly not likely to do so.

"Uh, Turk?"

I tried to look away. Nope, couldn't. Tried to close my eyes. Rats, welded open. Maybe I could just not listen. That didn't work either. Damn.

"Yeah, Harry?" Sounded like Turk was having the same problem as me.

"Could you please...uh...retrieve our pilot? I'm afraid my hands aren't working too well." It was true, and the proof was the rifle that lay at my feet. My rifle. I'd kinda dropped it.

"Sure, Harry." He handed his weapon over to one of his mates and gently disentangled Kik from the Shesharrian ambassador. It took much more time than I would have liked, but Shesharrians are very delicate, and hurting an ambassador is dangerous on many levels. Besides, it would be like crushing a butterfly, or kicking a cute puppy. Nobody could hurt a Shesharrian. They're just too beautiful.

It's hard for me to describe one, but they are slim, trilaterally symmetrical, and they have wings, the most beautiful multihued butterfly wings you've ever seen. And when they are...um...busy, they wrap their wings around their...um...partner, and don't let go very readily. They feel empathy through the touch of their wings, and the better you feel while they touch you, the better they feel. From the look of things, Kik was feeling *pretty* good.

Turk finally lifted her bodily out of the Shesharian's embrace and wrapped her in a robe. Her eyes opened slowly, a vacant look taking in the six armed men.

"Harry?" she said lazily. "What happened to your hair?"

"Long story. I had to pilot the *Limburger*. The planet's being bombed. We have to go."

"Bombed? Her eyes were starting to focus. "Who?"

"Farfnians."

"Mizz Kikira?" a lazy voice said. It was the Shesharrian. "What izz happening?"

"Oh, Riffy!" Her eyes snapped to needle sharpness. "Harry, we've got to take Riffy with us! He's alone here, and nobody's going to come pick him up for a month, and he has nobody, and he'll *die!*"

I'm such a sucker.

"We don't have time for this, Kik. Turk, bring the Shesharrian ambassador along."

"Fine!"

He snapped some orders to his mates, and two of them carefully helped the weak-kneed ambassador to his three shaky feet. Together we all worked our way back toward the *Limburger*. By the time we cycled the hatch closed, Kik was walking under her own power, albeit shakily. The Shesharrian looked fine, but what do I know about Shesharrians? He could have been breaking out in space-pox for all I could tell.

"Kik, to the bridge with me. Turk, I need you on tac. Have your men see our...guest to some secure quarters."

"Aye aye, sir."

"And no fraternizing!" I shot over my shoulder as I helped Kik to the lift.

We entered the bridge to see one very worried and one very elated face: Laila was worried. Zook was elated. I knew things weren't good.

"What's the news?" I asked, helping Kik to the pilot's couch.

"They've stopped bombing, anyway." Zook was scanning the tactical display.

"They're shooting at ships with nuclear missiles," Laila said flatly. "They're killing *thousands* of people!"

"Since when has that bothered a Farfnian?" I managed to keep most of the sarcasm out of my voice. "Though it does seem a little harsh for running cheese."

"It's not about cheese running, Harry," Laila said, pausing to trade a cool greeting with my pilot as I helped her out of her robe. A flight of icicles shot back and forth for a moment. "It's about something they're calling Tactics of Economic Destabilization. They shortened it to TEDs. They say the Carpoolians have been using TEDs to ruin the Farfnian economy, even threaten their home worlds. They are saying that this is a preemptive punitive measure."

"Yeah, punishment for making a profit." I was surprised that Turk grasped the situation so quickly. This had been building for years.

"Well, it's not our business anymore." I nodded to my pilot. "Get us the (**expletive deleted**) out of here, Kik."

"We're gone, Harry." I closed the lid of her couch.

The main drives blasted us off of the crumbling building even before I could sit down. Well, okay, that was partly because Laila was still in my chair, and I didn't think it would be appropriate to sit on her lap. I helped her to another seat and settled in. We were just breaking into the upper atmosphere when the proximity alarms went off.

"Turk?"

"I didn't see it! Some kind of stealthed interceptor ship. Small. It's on our tail, and it's shooting!"

The ship lurched, as if confirming his claim.

"Make sure Kik knows it's there!" We lurched sideways, rolling until the deck was the overhead. Thanks to whoever invented gravity inducers, we stayed in our seats.

"She knows!"

"Like, *duh*!" Laila's hands were white on her armrests.

We flipped and spun like a Frisbee™. Lockers were flung open by the jolt, and junk clattered across the deck. My stomach decided that I was going to be sick. My prosthesis argued. Brain argued with viscera for a moment.

"Hang on! She's going to—"

Turk didn't get a chance to finish his sentence, and I certainly didn't get a chance to tell him that I was already hanging on with every appendage that was designed by my maker to do so.

Kik spun the ship again, fired the atmospheric jets in reverse—we were still skimming along the ionosphere—and backed the ship right into our pursuer. An instant before impact, she fired the mains on full.

Damn, she's good!

A fusion engine is a poor weapon unless you're at point-blank range. The little ship simply ceased to exist.

"Nice move, Kik!" I shouted, knowing she couldn't hear. I thought about it for a second and asked, "Zook, can I plug in over here?"

"Oh, sure!" He vaulted out of his seat, bounced off of a few blunt stationary objects and skidded to a stop beside my chair. "Here!" He unwound a pair of thin wires from a pouch on his tool belt and plugged them into the arm of my chair; the other ends went into the back of my head.

The computer flashed into my mind.

"Nice move, Kik!" I said through the lines.

"Who the hell? Harry?"

"Yup! I learned a new trick from Zook. I can talk to you now while you're in the couch!"

"Fine. Don't bother me. I'm flying through a (**expletive deleted**) storm without a bucket!"

"Incoming!" That was Turk, and he sounded worried. "Missile tracking us! Closing fast!

"We've got a missile chasing us, Kik. Can you see it?"

"Nope!"

"Get us lined up for string insertion as quick as you can. Any string you can find."

"Thirty seconds!" Turk yelled. I wished he wouldn't yell. Turk peels paint when he yells.

"Five minutes to a string insert, Harry!"

That was not good news. I could have done the math with my

old brain!

"We're going to have to—"

Something hit us. I don't know what it was. Probably a beam weapon, maybe a piece of space debris, could have been my Aunt Martha for all I know. What I *do* know is that the ship skewed sideways like a drunk stepping off the curb by accident. Then I floated up out of my chair and drifted away from my controls.

The gravity inducers had failed.

I hate it a *lot* when the gravity inducers fail.

"Zook! Get the damned gravity back on!"

"Yep. Give me a minute."

"We're dead in twenty seconds!" I grabbed the wires that were plugged into my head and the chair and pulled gently. "Kik, we've got to—"

She hit the drive, and I drifted away.

The wires popped out.

She couldn't hear me, and didn't know we were about to be hit by a missile.

Turk was too busy at tactical to type in a message to her, and she was the only one who could shift the ship into stringspace. We were dead if she didn't do it in less than fifteen seconds.

This is what I call a *bad* day. And it had started out *so* good. Sometimes I think fate hates me.

I flailed toward my chair, but swimming through air is slow progress, and junk from the lockers kept bumping into me. Then something caught my eye—literally a glancing blow to my left eye—and I snatched it out of the air.

In my hand I held our salvation.

It was my can of Jiffy Whip™!

I pointed the can in the opposite direction of my chair and mashed on the squirter nipple. Emergency zero-gee propulsion in a can, and it tastes good, too. What more could you ask for?

I shooshed across the bridge leaving a contrail of whipped cream in my wake. I crashed into my crash couch with enough force to earn it its name, and snatched the wires that were my only connection to Kik. They snicked into place with a satisfying pop, and I apprised her of the situation.

"Kik, stringspace now or we're dead!"

"Harry, we're nowhere near an insertion line! We *can't!*"

I looked at Turk. His face was white. He was holding up five fingers, then four, then three...

"Kik," I said, trying for the right tone that would communicate our situation most precisely, "do it (**expletive deleted**) *now!*"

She did it.

We vanished on the crest of a thermonuclear explosion. To the rest of the universe, it must have looked like we'd been vaporized. That was fine by me. If they thought we were dead, they wouldn't come after us. We were safe. I started breathing again.

"Now *this* is interesting!"

Something in Zook's voice should have warned me. I looked up into the viewer. I had to check to make sure it was on. There was nothing outside.

Nothing.

No stars.

No planets.

Not even vacuum, if all the theories were right.

Yup, bad day all right...

I heard the ripping sound of the pilot's couch opening, but my eyes wouldn't leave the blank screen even for that.

"Where are we?" Laila asked. Her voice wavered. Maybe it was fear. If it was, she had company.

"Nowhere." That was Kik, and I was sure about the fear in her voice.

"Inter-string stringspace," Zook said reverently.

"So, how do we get back to regular space?" Laila asked in the same wavering tone.

"Can't."

"Why not?" Laila glared at Kik as if it were her fault.

"Because it doesn't work that way! We're stuck here." Kik sat down on the edge of her couch. "Forever."

"Forever?"

"Very interesting indeed," Zook said.
I can't say as I could agree with him.
"Well," Turk said, "we're alive, anyway."
Some consolation...

CHAPTER SIX

YO-YO

"Well, I always said I wanted to get away from it all." I tore my eyes away from the viewer and sat back down in my couch.

Nobody laughed.

Maybe nobody thought it was funny. Well, with all that *nothing* filling up the viewing screen, I didn't think it was very funny either. We were lost, quite literally, in the middle of nowhere. And there's nowhere quite as *no-where* as where we were, or weren't, because if this really was nowhere, we couldn't really be there, could we?

Uh-huh.

And we couldn't even ask directions. Well, maybe that was a good thing. Real captains don't ask directions, you know.

My scalp started feeling warm again.

I knew I couldn't stop thinking—obsessing I guess would be a better word—about all this, not without Zook doing some rewiring, so I settled for sitting back and putting everything into perspective, logically and rationally.

Well, it *could* happen...

Let's give it a try, shall we?

Think of stringspace as the interconnecting mesh that holds the universe together. Yes, I know the universe is expanding, but stringspace isn't, and no, I don't know why. In stringspace—which is itself a misnomer, since it's really not space at all—every body of significant mass—say, a solar system—is connected to all adjacent masses by graviton strings. Kind of like an extradimensional spider web. We travel from one solar system to the next by lining up on these strings, blinking into stringspace, and riding them. Like a yo-yo, forced to come back to the hand by the string it is riding; you can't get lost.

We had just made the jump without the benefit of a string, and much like a yo-yo without a string, the result was the same. We were lost in extradimensional non-space without a reference point. We couldn't go home. We were stringless; a yo without a yo to bring it back.

We were traveling—inertia is transferred with the jump—but it was impossible to say in what direction or how fast or far we were going. Since we weren't on a string, we had no way of getting back to regular space, and even if we could, there was no way to tell where we would blink in.

Space is mostly empty, which is why they call it "space", I suppose. Chances were about a billion to one that we would arrive in between stars, deep in interstellar space. We'd run out of fuel a thousand times if we tried to fly between two of the nearest stars in normal space.

My prosthetic brain was telling me all these things as I sat there staring at the black emptiness that filled the viewer—my eyes couldn't seem to stay away from it. I wasn't listening to my brain much, though. In fact, I was wondering if I could get Zook to turn it off for a while. I needed the rest.

"Harry?"

"Huh?" I looked at Laila. She looked a little shaken, maybe even stirred, too. Maybe her brain was as overloaded as mine.

"Thanks." One corner of her mouth quirked up a trifle, almost a smile. Considering the circumstances, I'd take any mirth I could get. "For saving my life, I mean."

"Oh, that." I waved a hand at the viewer and chuckled dryly. "Not much of a rescue, I'm afraid. Out of the microwave, into the Nuke-o-Matic®."

"Who *are* you, anyway?" Kik's tone wasn't exactly hostile, but neither is a porcupine.

"I'm...uh..."

"She's Laila, the ship's new Intragalactic Liaison Officer," I said, trying for a calming, authoritative tone. Uh-huh... Jello™

may as well have spewed from my mouth for all the calming effect it had.

"I'm a bartender." I gotta hand it to Laila, she said it like she was claiming a title as Queen of the Universe. And since we weren't exactly *in* the universe, maybe she was.

"A *bartender*?" Kik quirked an eyebrow, or would have if her eyes had brows, and looked around the bridge as if she'd misplaced something. "I don't see a bar. Are we going to install a bar on the bridge, Harry?"

"She helped save *your* life, Kik," I said, pushing myself up out of my couch. I didn't remember when the gravity inducers had come back on line. I guess my brain did a reboot about the time we left normal space. "You might lighten up a bit."

"Sorry," she said in a tone that stated flatly that she wasn't. "Thanks." That was directed more to me than Laila, and was equally flimsy.

"You're welcome," we both said. Synchronicity...wow. There was that crooked smile again. I returned it and started for the door.

"Where are *you* going?" Turk sounded worse than when we were being chased by a nuclear missile.

"Lunch."

"*Lunch?*"

"Yes, lunch, Turk. I'm starved, and I think better when my stomach isn't fighting for the same corpuscles that feed oxygen to my brain, okay?"

"I thought your brain was a computer."

Got me. Damn. When did Turk learn to think?

"Well, I need to eat anyway." So much for eloquence. "In fact, lunch is on me."

I went back to my chair and stabbed the little button on the armrest that opened the ship-wide intercom. "All hands, report to the mess hall." I stabbed another button. "Mishi, get out of the oven and whip up some lunch."

"Whip my rosy red—"

"Keep in mind that the refrigerated hold is empty, Mishi. It could be your new quarters if you're not careful."

"How about burritos!"

"Sounds good."

I wasn't lying about it sounding good; I didn't hire Mishi for his personality, after all. He's really a very good cook. I looked at my bridge crew and raised an eyebrow, then remembered that mine were as conspicuously absent as my pilot's.

"Who's hungry?"

Their enthusiasm was underwhelming, but they all followed me to the lift.

"Harry, could I just—"

"No, Zook, you can't."

"But it would be so..." His voice trailed off wistfully as the lift doors closed.

"Interesting?"

"Yes, interesting."

"I don't care if it would be interesting, Zook. You can't go outside."

"Okay. No harm asking."

"None at all."

Pathetic.

Lovable, but pathetic.

***

Mishi had really outdone himself. The burritos were spicy and wonderful, but conspicuously lacking in cheese; we'd used all our galley supply to buy off the Farfnian inspectors. To make up for its absence, I'd cracked open a few bottles of Herradura® blue agave tequila, and Laila was making margaritas.

My plan seemed to be working. Nobody appeared to be worried that we were hopelessly lost.

Most of the crew were sitting around talking to the Shesharrian ambassador, Riffy—he told me his real name, and I knew immediately why Kik called him Riffy. Riffy wasn't drinking, but then, he didn't need to; he had one wing around Kik's shoulder and another around one of the burly security guards. He would get an empathic buzz just from touching them, and could sober up instantly simply by breaking contact. I envied him on two counts: my prosthetic brain doesn't get drunk—you're buying me drinks because alcohol relaxes me, that's why—but I still get hangovers.

Just about anyone who wasn't clustered around the Shesharrian was talking about what had happened to the Carpoolians. Politics and alcohol are volatile enough on their own; put both in a blender and press "frappe", and something's liable to explode. Fortunately, everyone seemed to be on the same side here, which did nothing to reduce the volatility, but did reduce the chance of violence to a tolerable level.

Turk, surprisingly, was the center of the discussion. And, I had to admit, for a guy who generally thought that any interpersonal, interspecies, or intergovernmental problem could be solved by dislocating a few joints, breaking a few bones, or otherwise convincing his adversary that further conflict would be fatal, he was showing remarkable restraint.

He hadn't broken a bone yet.

On top of that, he was making an amazing amount of sense! Turk, talking in full sentences, some even with multi-syllable words. I'd never have thought he had it in him.

"But how could they justify genocide?"

That was one of the cargo handlers, arguing her point despite the veins bulging in Turk's neck. She either had guts or couldn't read the danger signs.

"What the hell does a crab care about killing a few million innocent people?" Turk punctuated his sentence not only with a question mark, but with a fist that nearly broke the table when he brought it down. "The Carpoolians finally undercut their profit margin enough to earn a butt kicking. With the War on Cheese heating up, Earth's probably next!"

"Bomb Earth?" The cargo handler downed the remnants of her margarita and shook her head. "They'll never do it. The crabs can't stand up against the whole *galaxy*!"

"They bombed Carpool!" Another fist to the table. One more

and I'd have to step in, if for no other reason than to save my furniture. "What makes you think they'll stop there?"

"Hey, simmer down, big guy!" Laila patted Turk on the shoulder and placed a fresh pitcher of margaritas on the table. "Let me refill that for you."

Turk simmered right down.

Amazing!

It's a wonder that bartenders don't rule the universe. Or maybe they do, and we're just a little slow on the pickup.

After diffusing the situation, Laila placed the half-empty pitcher—I told you I was a pessimist—on the table and sauntered—Yes, it was definitely a saunter. I was watching *very* closely—over to where I sat. Her quirky smile was intact, but I could see the worry under the façade.

"You don't like my margaritas?" She nodded to the bottle, salt shaker, and spent wedges of lime on the table before me.

"I get brain-freeze if I drink anything too cold." It wasn't exactly the truth, but the processor of my prosthesis does weird things with quick temperature changes, and I didn't particularly feel like breaking into show tunes.

"You mind?" She sat down and cut a wedge of lime.

"Please."

"Hold out your hand."

"Laila, I—"

"Shut up." She put the wedge of lime between my finger and thumb, then licked the back of my hand.

I shut up.

I have to admit, she *knows* how to drink tequila. The back of my hand still tingles when I think about it. But I couldn't let things get out of control.

"Laila," I started with all the conviction of an atheist in a confessional, "I can't..." It's hard to explain sometimes.

"Can't what? Let me thank you properly for saving my life?"

"Uh...yeah, that." She looked a little hurt, so I thought I'd better be more specific. "It's my brain, Laila. It can't...um..."

"Oh?"

"Exactly." She looked confused. "The "O" part. It's an amazing computer, but it can't...um...simulate certain functions."

"Oh, you mean you can't..."

"Oh, I can. The beginning part, at least. It's just the last part that doesn't happen."

"Oh!"

"Exactly."

"That must be..."

"Frustrating."

We stared at each other for a while, then she broke out laughing. This was the second time I thought she was finding mirth at my expense, and just as before, I was wrong.

"I'm sorry, Harry, but I've never met a man who was so immune to my charms before. You don't get drunk, and you don't...um..."

"Oh, I'm not immune." I joined in the laughter. It felt good.

"Immune to what?" Mishi trundled up and reached for my tequila bottle. I managed to rescue it from his grasp before it caught fire.

"Your manners!" I tucked the bottle away. "See if you can find some turpentine or something for Mish, will you, Laila?"

"Sure," she said with that same smile as she got up to find something combustible.

"So, what aren't you immune to?" Mishi edged away suspiciously. "I don't want to catch something from you if you're some kind of a *Typhoid Harry*."

"I'm not. And thanks for the lunch, Mish. The burritos were great."

"It's all in the sauce."

I didn't want to know what was in Mishi's sauce. Sometimes ignorance is safer, or at least more appetizing, than enlightenment.

"Glad you're not diseased." That was Mishi's idea of a compliment. "We don't have a doctor onboard, but I suppose we don't need one with Zook. It was pretty disgusting when he dug into the back of your head, you know."

"Sorry."

"No big deal. Hey, where is he anyway?"

"Over talking with the Shesharrian ambassador, I think." I glanced over, but couldn't spot his distinctive dark skin and hair.

"I walked right past both tables and didn't see him," Mishi offered. "I can't see very high, but he wears those funny sandals. You know the ones I mean."

"Nikenstocks™," I said, looking around again, a cold chill trickling down my spine.

"Yeah, those. Genuine endangered Carpathian boogie skin, made by hand by cloned juvenile Asoki slave laborers in China! Nice shoes!"

"I suppose," I said, not really paying attention. I raised my voice enough to be heard around the room. "Anyone seen Zook?"

The conversation died to some muttered claims that he'd left earlier.

"Did he say where he was going when he left?" I got to my feet; I didn't like this at all.

"Said something about getting some fresh air or something," one of the cargo-handlers said. "Didn't make much sense to me, but then he never does."

It made perfect sense to me.

That was when one of the alarm klaxons went off.

"Crap!" I raced to the panel to check, and my worst fears were confirmed.

Zook was indeed going for some fresh air, but I doubted he was going to find any outside the ship.

"I hope he put on a suit this time!"

I hit the general alarm and sprinted for the airlock.

CHAPTER SEVEN

TOO DARK

I guess there's a point in everyone's life when they forget about their own welfare and do something really stupid. Usually that's the end of that particular person's life, and natural selection has weeded out another "stupid gene" from the population. I wasn't thinking this when I arrived at the airlock. All I was thinking about was Zook.

Okay, so I'm a sentimental sap, but when someone saves my life, I take it seriously.

I could see him through the ridiculously small viewing port in the inner airlock door. He was standing by the outer lock—*sans* spacesuit, of course—and it was *open*.

Zook just stared at a wall of utter blackness outside the lock, his hands clenching and unclenching at his sides. I slammed my hand on the "Open" button, and the computer read my palm print, but the inner lock wouldn't budge when the outer one was open. *Damn factory-installed safety features!*

I stabbed the intercom button with my thumb and screamed, "Zook!"

"Yes, Harry?" He looked over his shoulder at me without turning around, as calm as if I was asking him to loan me a hundred dollars for a phone call. What? The price went up *again*? Damn inflation.

"Don't do it!" That's me, Mister Persuasive.

"Why not, Harry? It's very interesting. Watch." Zook poked a finger through the open portal and the blackness swallowed his whole hand. It was like he pushed into a wall of molasses. When he drew back, it stuck to him, then parted and bounced back and forth in slow-motion concentric ripples.

"See?" He looked over his shoulder at me and grinned. Some of the black nothingness had stuck to his hand, and it was dripping off in little globules that drifted about and sputtered black sparks as they dissolved into less than nothing. I stared for a moment as rapt as he, but my senses finally returned full force.

"No, Zook! It's no good!" I could hear the others running up, but I couldn't spare a glance to see who was there.

"No good? Why, Harry?"

"It's too dark!"

"Too dark?

"Yes, Zook! It's too dark out there!"

"But it's not dark, Harry. Dark is the absence of light, which is photons, which travel through space, which is only found in our universe. This isn't dark. It's just nothing. It's non-space-time."

"Just don't go out there! Please, Zook!"

"I'm sorry, Harry, but it's something that nobody's ever done before. Can you imagine? I could be the first being throughout the history of the universe!"

"Or you could be the last in a long line of dead idiots! Other ships have been lost in stringspace, Zook! They're all dead! Vanished forever!"

"Maybe, Harry." He took a half step forward and looked over his shoulder at me. He smiled that innocent, naïve-genius smile. "Or maybe they just went somewhere else. Somewhere...more interesting."

He took one step and vanished into the darkness.

I stared though the tiny port at the patch of blackness that had swallowed my friend. I would have said "Crap", but my brain and vocal cords had taken up their old feud again. If I was the melodramatic type, I would have screamed his name, burst through the door and rushed to the rescue. I'm more the silent idiot type. I just stared.

"Do *something*, Harry!"

I turned to see Kik staring at me, her eyes swimming with tears.

"What do you suggest?"

"Huh?" She looked at me, and I looked back. Two hairless faces blinking back at one another in blind panic.

"Should I go after him? Send out a search party? Beam down a security detachment? Fire phasers? What?"

"How can you joke about this?"

Okay, I was wrong about something earlier; Kik *can* look quite threatening when she wants to, and right now, hottiness or no, she looked like she was ready to rip my head off and use it for a Hacky Sack™. To avoid that less-than-delightful outcome, I opened my mouth to explain that my attempt at humor was not in any way an effort to make light of the current situation, but rather a poorly timed endeavor to diffuse the tension that we were all undoubtedly feeling at such a crucial juncture.

Unfortunately—or maybe fortunately—before I could say anything, something hit us.

Not just Kik and me, but the whole ship, and it hit hard enough to knock everyone to the deck. There were a lot of shouts, a few screams—no, not me, at least not that I recall—and a great number of thrashing arms and legs.

"What the hell was that?"

"Like I know?" I was a little tired of Turk thinking I had all the answers.

Something thumped against the other side of the airlock door as I struggled to my feet. I pressed my face to the glass, and was immediately crushed by the press of crewmen trying to do the same. I managed to get a glimpse of something black flopping around the floor.

I took the chance that it wasn't some horrible null-space alien trying to invade the ship and suck out all our brains—well, okay, maybe it was less of a risk to me than the rest of the crew—and finally took action.

"Gimme your gun, Turk!" I shouted.

"Huh?" Yep, he was back to the old Turk again.

"Give me your *gun!*" He didn't look armed, but I knew better. Turk wears a gun to bed, the shower, and while having carnal relations—don't make me explain how I know the last one. It was a safe bet that he was wearing one now.

"Uh, sure, Harry." He handed over a snub-nosed little blaster that would have leveled a small building. It would open the door nicely.

"Thanks." I thumbed the little "power" bar to full and aimed it at the airlock from about a foot away. "The rest of you might want to duck."

They ducked.

I fired.

The door went away.

We found Zook.

He didn't look good.

I'm through talking in single-sentence paragraphs now. Sorry.

Suffice to say that we, meaning myself and virtually the entire crew, pressed through the melted airlock door to aid our fallen comrade. It really only seemed like the whole crew, I guess, because the airlock is only about five-feet square, but it was crowded enough to make it uncomfortable, or very pleasant, depending on who you were pressed up against. I had Kik on one side, Turk on the other and Laila right behind, so it was about a thirty/sixty split.

Nobody rushed to grab Zook, however. He was covered in the black, sparkly un-space stuff that still filled the open airlock's outer door. My first thought was to help him, but he was thrashing around so badly that I couldn't get a decent grip on him. The stuff covering him was as slick as a lawyer's conscience, and about the same color.

Then Zook spoke.

Well, I thought it was Zook at first, but he wasn't making sense.

"**GO AWAY**!" it said. I say 'it' because I'm quite sure now that it wasn't Zook speaking. I really don't know what it was, but I know that it doesn't particularly like us—us meaning anyone from the normal space universe.

"Go away? What? Zook, can you hear me?" I tried to grab

him again and got a handful of nothing.

"**Do not touch. Go away! Go! Now!**"

Whatever it was, it was emphatic. I couldn't grab Zook, I couldn't communicate with whatever had him wrapped up like he'd been dipped in Teflon®, and I couldn't figure out what the hell to do! I often have that last problem, but the first two were new to me.

"It izz afraid."

I turned to the Shesharrian ambassador, Riffy, standing on the other side of Kik. His wings were folded tightly around him, giving him the appearance of a Technicolor® chrysalis, but his eyes were on Zook and he looked horrified.

"What?" Perfect question, right?

"It izz afraid of uzz, Captain Fizzhe." One wing waved at Zook, then recoiled. "I can feel itzz fear."

"Talk to it!" I pointed at the thing covering Zook as if there was any ambiguity as to who I thought he should talk to. "Touch it with your wings! Tell it to let him go!"

"No!" Riffy stumbled a step back. "I won't."

"You *will*!"

"You cannot order me, Captain Fizzhe."

"You haven't done a damned thing except my pilot to pay your way on this trip, Ambassador! If you don't try to save my friend, I think I'll consider you a stowaway and we'll see how well your wings work *outside*!"

I've never kicked a puppy or squashed a butterfly in my life, but right then I could have if it would save Zook's life. I think Riffy realized that. At least he did what I'd asked without arguing any more.

The Shesharrian knelt—Who knew he had knees?—and lay one multi-hued wing over the thrashing dark figure of Zook and whatever covered him. I guess I was expecting something more dramatic, but I can't say that I was disappointed with what *did* happen. The thrashing stopped, Riffy quivered like a leaf in the wind and unfurled his other two wings, and the black ooze that was really something—and nothing—else entirely, sloughed away from Zook until it was a puddle of emptiness on the deck around him.

Zook coughed roughly, and his voice came out scratchy.

"Now *that*,"—more coughing—"was interesting!"

Yep, that was Zook all right.

"I ought to kill you, you immortal twit!" I reached past Riffy and lifted Zook up by his shirt. His knees were a bit wobbly, so I wrapped my arms around him for some support.

Okay, it was a hug.

But it was a manly hug, and I'm not ashamed to admit it.

Besides, I don't think anyone was watching us. Everyone was watching Riffy, and with one glance I understood why.

"He's crying," Kik said, heartbreak edging her voice. She knelt beside the Shesharrian and put a hand on the frail shoulder that was heaving with sobs. "What's wrong, Riffy?"

"Zo zad," he said between sobs. One wing touched the dwindling puddle of nothing that darkened the floor. "It'zz dying."

"It's not dying, Ambassador." Zook let go of me—okay, we let go of each other—and reached down to brush the Shesharrian's wing. "Well, technically, it's dying, but it wasn't really alive. It's no more than an appendage. If I chopped off my finger and let it drop to the deck, the cells in it would live for a while. This's the same."

"The zame?" Riffy seemed to perk up at the news, or maybe Zook's perkiness was perking him up through his empathic wings.

"Yes, very much the same." Zook was standing on his own now and breathing almost normally. I just stood there and stared at him. "Stringspace is alive!"

Okay, he got my attention with that part.

"Alive?"

"Yes, alive." Zook waved at the emptiness of the airlock. "We're like an infection in its body. The strings we use for travel between stars are like its nervous system, for the lack of a better analogy. When we popped into interstring stringspace, we were treated like an infection. This," he waved at the dwindling puddle of nothing, "would be analogous to an antibody. It expelled me into the nearest convenient medium, and died after performing its purpose."

"So, is it going to dispose of us like an infection?"

That was Laila, and she sounded more scared now than I'd ever head her sound, and that included when we were about to be hit by a nuclear missile.

"It can't destroy us."

That was a relief. In fact, I don't think I've ever heard so many people heave a collective sigh before.

"It wants to expel us, push us out of its body, but it can't." He rubbed his chin and smiled that naive genius smile that I was learning to love. "It has, however, sent us home."

"Bull-(**expletive deleted**)." That sounded like Mishi, but I couldn't spot him thorough the crush of bodies to make sure.

"No. Really." Zook motioned to the almost gone puddle of nothing on the floor. "That was part of its function, to find out where I came from and return me there. I have taken on human form, right down to my DNA I might add, and it identified that as originating from Earth, and so, returned us there."

"Still looks as black as the ace of spades out there to me!" Yep, that was definitely Mishi.

"Oh, we're still in stringspace, Mishi. But we're in stringspace somewhere in the Earth system. I don't know how accurate their placement will be, but if we can shift into real space, I think we can make it."

"Oh, is that all?"

"Kik, I—"

"No, Harry," she said, using that threatening look again. Wow, twice in one day! "I'm not buying this. First he steps into null-space and gets puked back up like a bad oyster, and now he's telling us we're home when it looks suspiciously like wherever we were, or weren't, before! I think Zook's lost his mind! Besides, how are we supposed to get the ship back into normal space?"

"Oh, that." Zook looked a little embarrassed for the first time since I'd known him. "Well, I think if we energize the ship's outer hull with a negatively polarized graviton pulse it should—"

"Zook?" Yes, that was a very suspicious query.

"Uh, yes, Harry?"

"Have you always known how to shift the ship back into normal space?"

"Uh..." Zook edged a step back from the angry looks of the crew, and the captain, if the truth must be told. "Kinda."

"Kinda?"

"You rotten little immortal thrill-seeking..."

I put an arm out to keep Turk from, quite literally, killing our only hope of getting home.

"So." I tried to keep my voice level. "You could have brought us back into normal space at any time, right?"

"Uh, yeah, Harry. But we could have popped out anywhere! Deep in interstellar space, inside the corona of a star, even inside a planet!"

"So." Yep, level voice again. "You simply stepped outside to...ask directions?"

"Uh, kinda."

"Ummm, okay." I decided that real captains might, after all, require a discrete query regarding the referential position of the nearest celestial bodies. I turned to my crew and tried to assess their mood. From what I could tell, they were vacillating somewhere between homicidal rage and sphincter-cleansing relief.

"Well, however we may have achieved it, I believe we are about to be dumped right on our own doorstep." They didn't look like they were buying it, so I thought I'd state the plain facts and let them make the judgment. "Without Zook, we would have undoubtedly been lost in null-space forever, so I think we owe him at least a *little* thanks, right?"

There was a smattering of mumbled thanks directed at Zook. He took it very graciously, meaning he kept his fool mouth shut.

"There! See, that wasn't so bad, was it?" I should have taken a lesson from Zook. Most of the crew glared at me openly, the rest simply turned and left the proximity of the airlock.

"Good!" When in doubt, bluff, I always say! "Everyone to your stations, and Zook, please prepare whatever you need to bring the ship back into normal space."

"Uh, sure, Harry."

Everyone but my bridge crew and Riffy left for their stations. Kik, Turk, and Laila glared at me, though I fail to see how they could have been angry with *me*. Riffy simply clung to Kik like a piglet to the last available teat—okay, so maybe that's a bad analogy. Once again, I tried my old axiom concerning doubt.

"Did I just say '*To your stations*'?" I scratched the faint stubble on my chin, trying to look sarcastic, but more interested in the fact that my hair was coming back.

"Fine, but Riffy stays with me!" Kik flounced out, her rainbow-hued beau in tow.

"And give me my gun back!"

"Okay!"

I handed Turk his gun and headed for the door after my bridge crew, but Laila's soft, "Ah-hem," brought me back to the airlock.

"What?" I was a little tired of having my huevos scrambled, and a little ire had finally crept into my voice. "You want to chew off a piece of me now, too?"

"Um, not really," she said, surprising me with that same quirky smile that had melted my heart so many times, "though the prospect does have merit." Laila looked me up and down, and I got the distinct impression she was sizing me up for dinner. "But that can wait."

"Then what...?" Yes, bartenders *do* rule the universe, I'm sure of it.

"I just thought that you might want to shut the door." She nodded to the open outer airlock, still filled with an expansive view of nothingness.

"Oh, that." I walked casually over and palmed the door closed as if forgetting to do so would not have killed the entire crew upon our entry into normal space. "I was just seeing if you'd notice."

Yeah, right. Like I could fool the Queen of the Universe.

CHAPTER EIGHT

HOME AGAIN, HOME AGAIN, JIGGITY JIG

It took Zook about half an hour to get everything ready to drop the ship out of stringspace into normal space. That was just as well. After a few rounds of Laila's margaritas, everyone needed a little time to sober up. I cracked open a box of Alco-seltzer™ and ordered it passed around. The *Limburger* was bristling with instant hangovers in a matter of minutes. Leave it to a pharmaceutical company to cure drunkenness, but not the aftermath. Rather like curing heart disease but leaving the chest pain, I think.

My major concern—besides having a crew that looked like they'd been embalmed—was exactly where we would re-enter normal space. It was likely that the *Limburger* had been reported destroyed while fleeing Carpool Prime. If we simply popped in among the regular clutter of space traffic near Earth, we might be able to slip through the orbital sentries and land unnoticed. If we arrived at one of the usual string debarkation lanes, we would have to go through customs and immigration, and therefore answer a lot of questions regarding exactly why we hadn't been vaporized. Not to mention the fact that I had an unregistered clone and an illegal alien aboard, even if he was an ambassador.

These were questions that I didn't particularly want to answer.

I'd queried Zook on the matter of our re-entry, but he didn't have any specifics for me. It seems that his rather short relationship with the null-space antibody—for wont of a better term—had only given him the impression that he'd been sent home. He did tell me that the blob of black goo that had enveloped him was as sentient as you or me, though it was, in essence, just a tiny bit of the greater organism of stringspace. It made my scalp tingle to think of a creature so beyond us that its every cell was as smart as me. It also made me start wondering about things like the origin of the universe, something that I usually don't wonder about, being a devout agnostic.

My scalp was so warm that my newly sprouting follicles were screaming in pain, so I decided to occupy myself with something less demanding. Since mind-numbing chemicals have little effect on me, and we didn't have a television, I decided that some light conversation was in order. My usual bridge crew didn't look up to the task—aside from being hung over, Kik was pissed at me and busy nuzzling with Riffy, and Turk was...well, Turk—so I thought Laila might like to chat.

"So, Laila," I said, exhibiting my usual suave repartee, "who was your owner on Carpool?"

"I thought you knew!" She looked a little surprised.

"Nope, not a clue."

"Neezl. Who else?" I gave her my best '*Huh?*' look, so she enlightened me. "What kind of Carpoolian would give you a lift to a bar it *didn't* own, Harry?"

"Oh." Put that way, it was obvious. Then a thought struck me. "But it saw you! You talked to it when we were looking for Kik!"

"So?"

"So, it must think I *stole* you!"

"No, it doesn't."

"Why not?"

"Don't you remember?" I shook my head, indicating that I had no idea what she thought that my infallible memory had failed to record on its limitless hard drive. "You said you'd send my owner a money-o-gram. You bought me free and clear, Harry. The bill of sale was logged and everything."

"When?"

"Well, while I talked to Neezl."

"Neezl took the time to file a bill of sale while the planet was being *bombed*?" Then I realized that I was talking about a Carpoolian. Laila must have seen that recognition on my face, because she didn't reply. I rubbed my warm scalp and said, "But I don't *want* to own you!"

"You don't?" Laila's face fell like a soufflé at a kettle-drummer convention.

Damn. Maybe I *should* take up kicking puppies and squashing butterflies; I seem to be good at it, anyway.

"I don't want to *own* you, Laila. I want you to be free."

"I thought you *liked* me."

Hmm, let's see if I can fit *both* feet in my mouth now. "I *do* like you, Laila. But you're a sentient being; nobody should own another sentient being. It's slavery."

"But the law says—"

"I don't give a flippin' Farfnian fart what the *law* says, Laila!" I bit my lip and made a decision. "I'll pay Neezl, but as far as you and I are concerned, you're your own woman as of right this second!"

"I am?" Her face started to register something besides shock and pain, so I guessed that I was on the right track.

"Yep. And you're also a paid member of this crew! So when we hit dirt, you've got a paycheck coming!"

"I do?" We were back in smile mode now. Mission accomplished!

"Yep. Only half a share, since you didn't make the trip out, just the one back, but it'll be quite a lump considering what we took Neezl for."

"Oh, about that, Harry." She bit her lip, reverting back to "worried, but cute".

"About what?"

"Um, I didn't have much time, and Neezl wasn't going to haggle, and with Kik's life in the balance, I thought it best if I just wrapped the deal up."

"Deal? What deal?"

"Me."

My poor overworked prosthesis finally managed to put two and two together and get an even sum. My scalp prickled and it had nothing to do with the itchy stubble that was trying to grow before it died of the heat. Maybe I should stay bald.

"How much to I owe Neezl, Laila?"

"Half."

"Half of my cut? That's a lot of money, but I think I can—"

"No, Harry. Half of the whole payoff. Fifty million farfs."

"You're kidding." Having your heart stop beating twice in as many days can't be healthy. Maybe Zook could fit me with a prosthetic. One look at Laila's face told me that she was most definitely *not* kidding. "Crap."

"Sorry, Harry. I didn't mean to—"

"Forget it." I waved a hand and smiled, deciding that I would burn that bridge later. "The deal can't be binding, anyway. There must be a law somewhere about verbal contracts with persons not wielding proper power of attorney during alien invasions and asteroid bombings. In fact, I think there's a precedent-setting case, Godzilla versus Megalon or something like that. It doesn't matter."

I heard the lift doors open and Zook's cheerful, "Okay! We're ready to shift into normal space, Harry. Everyone ready to go home?"

"I can't think of a place I'd rather be, Zook." I thumbed the switch that opened the shipwide intercom and said, "We're about to be home, ladies and gents, so hang on to your Cheese Whiz™!" I let up on the button and said, "Kik, get ready. I want to be ready to scoot if we blink into the wrong backyard. You, too, Turk. Full tactical scans."

"But what about the money, Harry?"

Great! Turk wasn't only learning how to think, but also how to eavesdrop.

"Don't worry about it!" I glared at him so hard that I neglected to stare at my pilot as she dropped her jumper and climbed into the pilot's couch. Okay, so I was *really* distracted. "As far as Neezl knows, we were vaporized. And if it does find out we're alive, and doesn't nullify the bill of sale and settle for a reasonable price, we'll take our cheese elsewhere."

"Ready, Harry?" Zook was strapped into his couch with his finger poised over a button.

"Hang on." I activated my own crash restraints—when Zook starts being careful, I get nervous—and gave him the nod. "Okay,

Zook. Let's see where we are in real space."

He pushed the button and the darkness filling the viewer vanished.

***

"Looks like Topeka."

The viewing screen was filled with the grill and windshield of a semi tractor-trailer bearing down on us. It was an impressive sight, made more so by fact that the driver was slamming on the reverse thrusters and the emergency impact retarders—brakes, if you're from that era—hitting the air horn and giving us the finger all at the same time. I had guessed Topeka simply from the large *Kansas* license plate affixed squarely in the center of the huge front bumper.

He managed not to hit the *Limburger*, for which I will always be thankful—he would have scratched the paint for sure—but for some reason, after all that had happened on this trip, materializing into normal space in the middle of a busy intersection seemed rather anticlimactic.

"Des Moines, I think," Zook said. "Must be out-of-state plates."

"Why?" I heard the pilot's couch open, but once again, I was too numb to care.

"Just guessing, but I think that whatever put us here is very precise. Unless I'm mistaken, this is the exact street corner where I originally took human form." Zook pointed to a store front. "Right over there."

"You mean, whatever moved us halfway across the spiral arm managed to put you within fifty feet of where you originated?"

"Yup."

"Nice shooting." Turk's tone was appreciative, but as burned out as the rest of ours.

"What do you want me to do, Harry?" That was Kik, leaning out of the pilot's couch—okay, I tore my eyes away from the viewer for a quick glance—with a disgusted look on her face. She was probably disappointed that, this being a spaceship, we didn't arrive in space, and therefore didn't get to endure another of her hair-raising re-entry maneuvers.

"Can you take off without melting any buildings?"

"Sure."

"Get us a little altitude then, please. As soon as we're out of town, stay low. We don't want to get picked up by the orbitals." The crabs watch us pretty closely—cheese interdiction is a multi-billion-farf industry—but they can't track every sub-orbital passenger carrier, and that's what we would look like if we stayed low and slow. "Then you can proceed to our destination, but keep it below shockwave speed, huh?"

"Wisconsin in an hour, Harry." Kik sealed her couch and we rumbled into the air. The angry trucker gave us another bit of sign language and pulled his huge rig back onto the street.

"Harry?"

"Yes, Laila?" She was looking at a number of blinking lights on her board with a curious look on her face. "What's all this?"

"Oh, I piped all the communications to you. Those are incoming calls. The yellow ones are Earth origin. Looks like they're all yellow. That's good. Just answer and tell them we had a slight navigational error. Mention the name of the ship; that should put them off. If any red ones pop up, those are from orbit. Don't answer those."

"Uh, okay." She got busy, just like she'd been doing it all her life. Best damn intragalactic liaison officer I ever had. Okay, so she was the first I ever had, but she's still the best! Best *officer*, I mean. No, *really*! Fine, think what you want, but keep it clean, huh?

We'd been slugging along at just under the speed of sound at about a thousand feet for almost an hour when Turk broke the blissful silence with an expletive that truly shocked me. Suffice to say that he got my attention, if not my approval.

"What is it, Turk?"

"Explosion in low orbit. Looks like one of a squadron of sprayers; the others are peeling out of formation. Wreckage is coming down."

"Damn!"

This was all we needed! The Farfnians had been spraying anti-bovine retroviruses for almost a decade. The Hindu Underground Bovine and Cattle Advocacy Police—unfortunate acronym, I know—had been sabotaging them for about the same. The former wasn't really doing much to impede the production of cheese, since all our production facilities were atmospherically isolated, but it made the Farfnians and their bought-and-paid-for human conspirators feel like they were doing something constructive. The latter just added violence to the equation and gave honest cheese runners a bad name. This particular attack was just about to land right in our front yard, and might draw far too much attention to us.

"How close?"

"To us? Not very." I gave Turk a look that told him that I knew he knew what I really wanted to know. "Might hit close enough to The Barn to do some damage, though."

"The Barn?" That was Laila, looking confused. I noticed her board was lit up with several red lights now. That wasn't good.

"Home base, Laila." I nodded to her board. "There are probably some emergency transmissions in that mess. See if you can listen in. Turk, give me some data on the impact."

"Sure, Harry." He sounded bored. Of course, that was in comparison to what he sounded like when we were being bombed, boarded, blitzkrieged, and blasted into alternate universes. Maybe he *was* bored.

I took the wires out of my pocket and plugged myself into the computer so that I could talk to Kik.

"Kik, you see that debris falling?"

"Uh, no, Harry...I thought it was just *raining* burning bits of aircraft."

"Fine. Just try to avoid it, then. I didn't pack my umbrella." I pulled the wires, having had my daily recommended allotment of sarcasm already this morning. Too much gives you cavities, you know.

"Looks like impact in about two minutes, Harry." Turk shrugged his massive shoulders and yawned. "Gonna miss The Barn by about two klicks. We can get there before it hits."

"But *should* we?"

The crash was going to draw attention, and I didn't particularly want to be around to deal with that. Ask anyone who's ever done anything illegal; the last thing you want while in the act is attention. Not that we were currently committing a crime, but if we got caught up in the middle of this there would be all those questions that I was talking about earlier. Oh, and the hundred-million farfs that was stashed in the secret hold. Yeah, there was that. I mulled over a few alternatives for conversations with the Farfnian crash-investigation team in my head. Unfortunately all of them ended with, "Oh, *that* hundred-million farfs! I have no idea where *that* came from!" and me being hauled off to jail, forever.

The alternative was to disappear. That would risk the whole Wisconsin operation, but then, so would me going to jail. I'm not saying that I would sing like a canary, squeal like a pig, or otherwise perform animal impressions, but I value my hide a lot. I decided to follow the tried-and-true method that has kept me alive and free so far throughout my somewhat tarnished life: run away and hide.

"Laila, open a frequency at exactly 3.1415927 terahertz and broadcast this 'Home again, home again, jiggity jig.'"

"Easy as pi."

I looked at her incredulously, and she smiled back as she transmitted the signal. No wonder they cloned this woman! I plugged back into the computer and told Kik, "The door's open. Hit it."

"Okay, Harry, but tell everyone to hang on. At this speed, even the broad side of a barn is hard to hit!"

"I've got the utmost trust in your piloting abilities, Kik. You know that." I pushed the Fasten Seatbelts and Return To Your Seats buttons, knowing that Kik couldn't see what I was doing. Not that being tied down would be any safer if we hit a solid wall at Mach one.

"Yeah, right." If her tone was any indication, maybe she *could* see what I was doing. That was disconcerting.

"Everybody hang on," I said quite unnecessarily as The Barn came into view on the horizon.

The Barn is just that, a huge red wooden structure sitting behind a pastoral-looking farmhouse. It's all a sham, of course. A front for the entrance to the Wisconsin Cheese Factory. Still, it looked peaceful. Hopefully it would stay that way.

Kik dropped the ship to treetop level and aimed straight at the side of the barn.

"Harry? What are we—"

"Don't worry, Laila. It's a hologram. If we hit it just right, we'll be fine."

"Debris is just about to hit, Harry," Turk said, confirming my suspicion that he was still doing his job.

"Good. Everyone will be looking at that and not us."

The Barn grew in the screen until it filled it, and I tried not to break the armrests of my crash couch as we passed through the hologram at the speed of sound.

Kik slammed on the vertical thrusters, changing our course to thirty degrees down in the blink of an eye. I swallowed my stomach, happy that we had not been killed—yet—and that I was the only one on the bridge who hadn't voiced his or her concern and or amazement. Okay, Laila and Riffy screamed, Turk "Hooooaaa'ed" and Zook said, "Can we do that *again*?!"

"Maybe later, Zook," I said, trying to sound calm—uh-huh. The florescent lighting strips of the launch tunnel were whipping past at an alarming rate even though Kik was braking hard. The hanger was at the end of the tunnel, and was usually very crowded. Flying into it at this speed would be disastrous if anything was in our way. "I hope nobody took our parking spot!"

Black and yellow warning stripes indicating the end of the tunnel flashed past so fast that I thought a giant space bumble bee had attacked the ship. Don't laugh, that happened once. We passed the threshold at about a hundred KPH, and Kik did something that I would have never thought possible. She hit the lifters in a pulse that nudged the ship straight up about sixty feet, just enough to clear the row of parked ships that crowded the hanger floor.

In fact, we missed by such a close margin that a mechanic standing atop a ship working on an antenna array flattened himself to avoid being chopped off at the waist by our intake manifold.

Unfortunately, the antenna he was working on was clipped off and sucked in. The antenna wasn't large, but it was metal, and when metal is sucked into a jet engine, bad things happen.

The *Limburger* shuddered like an albatross that had swallowed a bad herring.

"Oh crap!" I stared at Zook in amazement. I'd never heard him say such a thing.

"Zook? What—"

Something went *WHUMP* deep within the bowels of the ship. It was definitely a *WHUMP*, and definitely in the bowels, not the stomach, nor the duodenum, but the bowels. How did I know? I knew because I'd switched the viewer to aft so that we could look behind us, and the *Limburger* was literally pooping out a trail of flaming engine parts from the atmospheric jet exhausts.

"Flameout!" Zook yelled—that was also the first time I'd heard him yell—and stabbed the controls that would turn off the fuel supply to the engines.

"Kik!" I yelled mentally, intending to inform her that our primary atmospheric engines were about to be turned off, leaving us without any way to stop the ship except maneuvering thrusters. I didn't have time to say all this, of course, since the end of the hanger was quickly approaching, and reinforced concrete would probably stop us much more effectively than the thrusters.

"Got it, Harry!"

That was Kik and, as usual, she was way ahead of me.

Let me explain something before I tell you exactly what happened.

The main fusion drives of a stringship are not designed to be used when the ship is near the surface of a planet. It says so right in the manual. When I used them on Carpool, melting a few buildings in the process, it was in violation of about a dozen laws of navigation, a few intragalactic edicts, and at least one commandment. To fire the main engines *inside* a structure like a hanger, for instance, is sheer insanity.

Did I mention that my pilot is insane?

She fired the starboard engine—just a puff, really, and I didn't see anything melt in the rear view mirror, so maybe she wasn't *that* insane—and the ship spun like one of those whirly firecrackers I mentioned way back. When we had swung around so that we were pointing the opposite direction she fired again, exactly the same puff, this time on the port engine, then hammered both just enough to stop us dead in the air.

Of course, without the atmospheric jets we couldn't stay aloft, so the ship fell about sixty feet to the solid concrete floor—into the only available parking space in the hanger.

Quite a jolt. Especially since the landing gear wasn't down.

Remind me to check my insurance policy.

"Well, we're home," I said, pushing myself up from my crash couch. I was feeling rather good about myself at that point. Everyone was alive, the ship was intact if somewhat dented, and we had brought home the biggest single payoff in the history of cheese running.

I stepped over to the pilot's couch as it opened and helped Kik out, my eyes firmly riveted to hers as I said, "Kikira, you are without a doubt the best pilot in the Milky Way." I then placed a firm kiss right on her lips.

I never asked her if she enjoyed it or not, but she didn't slap me or anything, so it couldn't have been that bad.

"Laila," I said, leaving my pilot to the Technicolor™ embrace of her Sheesharian beau, "could you come with me please?"

"Uh, sure, Harry." She put her hand in mine and I headed for the exit.

"Oh, and Zook, could you come along, too?"

"Uh, I don't know if I want two of—"

"Relax, Laila, I've got some programming for him to do, that's all."

"Oh!"

"Exactly." I looked to my immortal friend. "Well?"

"Sure, Harry!" He smiled, got up and followed us out.

***

About an hour later, after some minor reprogramming and a little bit of "software testing," Laila and I left the ship.

The *Limburger* was standing on her landing struts now, albeit a bit wobbly, and the loading platform was down. I don't remember the ship moving, or perhaps I do, but I thought it was the Earth moving at the time. Zook is *quite* a programmer.

Anyway, when we descended to the platform, the entire Wisconsin Cheese Fleet was there to greet us. Captains, officers, and crew of over forty other ships shook our hands, hugged us, and handed us drinks. That was kind of redundant for me, since I was about as relaxed as I could get. It *had* been a long time.

There was quite a party going on. Alice Vanderbilt, captain of the good ship *Gouda*, and George Hong, pilot of the *Emmenthaler*, grabbed me and led a resounding cheer of "Hail to the Cheese." The crates of Farfnian currency were being unloaded, and the paymaster was ticking off the riches on his ledger. We had made our run and in record time, thanks to a little detour into inter-string stringspace.

Zook was there and looked to be actually enjoying himself, telling stories about his unique experiences. Turk was gesticulating wildly as he told of the firefights, star battles and being chased by a nuclear missile. Mishi was cuddling with his wife, Moshi—I didn't tell you he was married? Oh, well, he is, and her temper makes his look like a candle next to a supernova—and the two were generating enough heat to jumpstart a fusion reactor. Riffy was the center of a crowd of excited xenophiles—Kik's friends—and they were all conspicuously brushing accidentally against his wings, even though Kik was clinging to him, looking possessive.

So, anyway, that just about wraps it up. But that run was a piece of cheesecake compared to our *next* one!

Buy me another drink, and I'll tell you all about it.

Record # KR29387/a. Transcript ends.

We hope you are enjoying the Cheese Runner's Trilogy

Cheese Runners
Cheese Rustlers
Cheese Lords

Available in audio, electronic, and print formats

About the Author

From the sea to the stars, Chris A. Jackson's stories take you to the far reaches of the imagination. Raised on the back deck of a fishing boat and trained as a marine biologist, he became sidetracked by a career in biomedical research, but regained his heart and soul in 2009 when he and his wife Anne left the dock aboard the 45-foot sailboat *Mr Mac* to cruise the Caribbean and write fulltime.

With his nautical background, writing sea stories seemed inevitable for Chris. His acclaimed Scimitar Seas nautical fantasies won three consecutive Gold Medals in the ForeWord Reviews Book of the Year Awards. His Pathfinders Tales from Paizo Publishing combine high-seas combat and romance set in the award-winning world of the Pathfinder Roleplaying Game. Not to be outdone, Privateer Press released *Blood & Iron*, a swashbuckling novella set in the Iron Kingdoms.

Chris' repertoire also includes the award-winning and Kindle best-selling Weapon of Flesh Series, the contemporary urban fantasy *Dragon Dreams*, as well as additional fantasy novels, the humorous sci fi Cheese Runners trilogy of novellas, and numerous short stories.

To learn more, please visit jaxbooks.com.

From Paizo Publishing
Pirate's Honor
Pirate's Promise
Pirate's Prophecy
Pirate's Curse (early 2017)

From Privateer Press
Blood & Iron (ebook novella)

From the Ed Greenwood Group
Hellmaw: Dragon Dreams

Check out these and more at
jaxbooks.com

Want to get an email about my next book release?
Sign up at http://eepurl.com/xnrUL